THE BEAR WHEELED AND
STARTED BACK TOWARD NATE...

At any second Silver Hair would spot Nate, and in its agitated state, the grizzly would charge whether it detected his scent or not. Nate turned to the cliff and saw numerous spots where the rock face had crumpled. Climbing the rock wall was his only hope. If he could get high enough, the grizzly wouldn't be able to get him. Wedging his fingers into a narrow cleft, he rose a few inches. He dared not glance over his shoulder. The delay might cost him his life.

Five feet he climbed. Then seven. His fingers hurt, his toes too, but he couldn't slow down. He expected to hear the monster closing on him, but heard nothing. Then, as he grabbed for a hole formed when some of the stone had eroded away, he heard a rumbling growl from directly below, and peering between his legs, Nate saw Silver Hair at the base of the cliff. That very instant, the bear lunged upward, its huge forepaw reaching up to rip him from his perch....

The *Wilderness* series published by *Leisure Books:*

WILDERNESS

Blackfoot Massacre

David Thompson

LEISURE BOOKS   **NEW YORK CITY**

To Judy, Joshua, and Shane.

A LEISURE BOOK®

August 1992

Published by

Dorchester Publishing Co., Inc.
276 Fifth Avenue
New York, NY 10001

Printed in the United States of America.

Chapter One

The strapping young man in fringed buckskins sighted down the barrel of his heavy Hawken rifle, his striking green eyes narrowing as he aimed at the buffalo cow grazing contentedly 20 yards off. From his prone position on a grass-covered knoll he could see her great jaws moving as she munched and the flick of her short tail as she lazily swatted at circling flies. His thumb curled around the metal hammer and pulled it back until he heard a click.

What a stroke of luck! Nate King reflected. To have stumbled on a lone cow so soon after beginning his hunt meant he would be back with his wife and son much sooner than he had anticipated. He would have liked to bring the boy along, but the only time Zach got to mingle with their kin and frolic with other children was for three or four weeks each spring when the family visited the Shoshones and for a brief spell at the annual Rendezvous. So rather than interrupt his son's fun, he'd gone hunting alone.

Nate absently wondered why the cow was alone as he

prepared to squeeze the trigger. Ordinarily, buffalo congregated in large herds, and he had been following a clear trail left by hundreds of the dumb brutes when he spotted the cow. Perhaps she was lame. Or maybe she had simply wandered off from the main body. Whatever the case, he wasn't about to pass up this golden opportunity.

Although buffalo were notoriously difficult to dispatch with a single shot, at such short range he was confident of dropping her with one ball to the heart. Having butchered scores of buffalo since leaving New York City nine years ago for the rugged life of a free trapper in the majestic Rocky Mountains, he knew precisely where a buffalo's vital organs were located.

Nate grinned, thinking of how amazed Winona would be to see him back at the Shoshone village so soon, and lightly touched his forefinger to the trigger. Taking a breath, he steadied the Hawken, and was all set to fire when the high grass near the cow stirred and up stood a young calf.

Blinking in surprise, Nate watched the reddish calf wobble over to its mother's side and bawl to get her attention. It was a newborn! Now he understood why the cow was by herself. She must have stopped to deliver her offspring, and the herd had continued on to the south, leaving her behind. In a day or two, when the calf was strong enough, she would catch up with the main body.

Damn! Nate fumed in annoyance, lowering the gun. This changed everything. While there were some mountain men and any number of Shoshone warriors who would kill both mother and calf without hesitation, regarding both as nothing more than food on the hoof, shooting either now went against his grain. Others might laugh and call him soft, but he couldn't bring himself to slay a mother and her baby, even if they were only animals.

Carefully lowering the hammer, Nate observed the calf greedily sucking milk from the cow's teats. Then he eased backward on his elbows and knees and angled down the knoll until he could stand without being seen by the mother buffalo. His proximity to the calf might cause her to charge, forcing him to shoot her whether he wanted to or not.

Turning, Nate walked to his splendid stallion, a gift he had received at a recent rendezvous from the Nez Percé after he helped them fight the dreaded Blackfeet. Widely noted for their horsemanship, the Nez Percé were also regarded as the best horse breeders west of the broad Mississippi. Many frontiersmen would give a year's earnings just to own one of their outstanding animals. His stallion was typical of the breed; it sported black spots on a roan background, had white-rimmed eyes, and was further distinguished by white stripes over its hoofs.

He swung nimbly into the saddle, gripped the reins, and swung around, about to head northward in search of more buffalo. In the far distance, at the limits of his vision, something moved, a tiny black speck amidst the vastness of the unending prairie. Leaning forward, he placed his left hand over his eyes to block out the bright morning sun. Was it another buffalo? If so, he'd reach the Shoshone village by dark and spend all night with his wife. The appealing prospect brought a smile to his lips.

Playing it safe, Nate turned to the west and rode in a wide loop in the hope he would spot a low hill or another knoll from which he could spy on whatever it was. While he would much rather ride in a beeline and find out if it was indeed a bull so he could kill it and return to the village, prudence dictated otherwise. As he well knew, careless mountaineers did not survive long in the wilderness. One of the first laws of survival he had learned was to never take anything for granted. What if that moving dot was in reality a fierce grizzly or a hostile warrior? He must determine what it was before he made his presence known.

He hunched low over the saddle to blend his silhouette with that of the stallion's. From far off the horse would appear to be riderless, just one of the many wild animals roaming the plains. If that figure out there was indeed an enemy, a lone horse wouldn't arouse suspicion.

Nate held the Hawken in his right hand, the reins in his left. He could feel the twin flintlocks he invariably carried rubbing against his midsection. They were wedged tight under his brown leather belt, one on either side of the big buckle. In addition to the pistols, he had a butcher knife in a beaded sheath on his left hip and a tomahawk tucked under the belt above his right hip. Slanted across his broad chest were a bullet pouch and a powder horn. Moccasins covered his feet. In every respect his attire was typical of trappers, those hardy souls who had ventured into the remote vastness of the foreboding Rockies to make their living by securing beaver pelts for the lucrative Eastern and European markets.

Nate had never regretted his decision to come west. Not only had he found the love of his life in the beautiful person of Winona, he had also discovered the true meaning of a word he had never paid much attention to during the years he spent growing up in New York City, a word he now regarded as one of the most precious in the entire English language: freedom. To be able to live as he pleased without being accountable to any man meant as much to him as life itself. Back in New York, where he had bowed to his father's every whim and labored as an aspiring accountant under a spiteful taskmaster, he had been bound by invisible chains and never realized the fact. His behavior had been . . .

What was that?

Nate drew rein, listening to the mournful, wavering notes of an eerie howl that wafted on the cool breeze. He glanced toward the dot, squinting in an effort to see it better. The distance prevented him from being certain, but he had the impression the figure was walking on two legs. A man afoot? It must be an Indian since no white man in his right mind would dare be so foolhardy as to travel anywhere in the wilderness without a horse. There were too many dangers, from wild beasts and hostiles alike.

The howling was repeated, and to the east of the lone figure materialized a dozen or more low forms flowing over the ground in the figure's direction.

Nate straightened, the short hairs at the nape of his neck tingling. Those forms were wolves. Although they ordinarily gave humans a wide berth, they would attack if hungry enough or if they came on an injured man or woman incapable of offering much resistance. They did the same with buffalo. Wolves were Nature's way of gleaning the weak and the aged from the huge herds, of insuring only the fittest survived. Elk, deer, and smaller game also fell prey to the roaming packs.

"Let's go, Pegasus," Nate said, goading the stallion into a gallop. An avid reader, he had always been fond of the many tales about ancient Greek heroes. As a child he had delighted in the fantastic exploits of the winged steed Pegasus. So when the Nez Percé had presented the stallion to him, the finest horse he had ever seen, he had named it after the mythical mount of antiquity.

"Faster," Nate urged. He had fallen into the habit of talking to the horse as he often did to the family dog, Samson. Some of his trapper friends thought he was mad. Why get attached to an animal, they often argued, when one day he might have to eat it? A valid point, but he still regarded Pegasus and Samson more as loyal friends than mere domesticated beasts. The dog had many times proven itself by saving him and his loved ones, and the horse had yet to fail him in time of need.

Now Pegasus flew, its mane flying, its sleek body rippling with latent power. Nate rode expertly, his gaze on the wolves. He guessed they were still a quarter of a mile from the man. If he rode hard he might be able to intercept them.

The wolves of the western lands were particularly hardy specimens. While not quite as large as their kin in the Atlantic states, they were thickly made and endowed with tremendous stamina and strength. Their color was usually a gray or blackish-brown, although some were occasionally seen that were a cream-colored white. Working in concert, they could pull down a grown buffalo bull or an elk with deceptive ease.

Nate wondered why the wolves' quarry made no effort to run. Surely the man could hear the howling. As he drew nearer, he discovered he had been wrong about the figure's identity. It was a white man, not an Indian, dressed in black pants, a white shirt, and a black coat. He also noticed the man walked slowly, unsteadily, with head bowed, and figured the poor soul must be injured or ill, which explained why the pack had given chase.

He hefted the Hawken, calculating the range, certain he could down one or two if he was to stop and take careful aim. But the rest would probably press on and overwhelm the man. If he was to do any good, he must get between the wolves and their prey.

The man suddenly turned, saw the pack, and broke into an ungainly run, his right arm pressed to his chest as if he were in great pain. But instead of heading south, toward Nate, he raced westward in stark panic.

"Here!" Nate shouted. "This way!"

Looking around at the sound, the man spied Nate and instantly changed course, his legs pumping furiously. "Help!" he cried weakly. "Please help me!"

I'm trying to, Nate reflected grimly. Some of the wolves had seen him and stopped. Eight continued to close on their intended victim. In the lead was an enormous gray wolf bearing a black mark on its forehead.

The man glanced at his pursuers, failed to watch where

he was going, and tripped when his right boot snagged in a clump of grass. He stumbled and fell, landing on one knee, his right arm tight against his chest.

Snarling viciously, the lead wolf was almost upon him.

Nate let go of the reins and whipped the Hawken to his shoulder, using the pressure of his legs to stay astride Pegasus. He took a hasty bead, keenly aware of the consequences should he miss, and got off a shot just as the lead wolf leaped. Fate smiled on him, for the wolf reacted as if struck in the side by a mallet, twisting in midair and flopping over to crash onto the ground and lie still.

Undaunted, five of the pack were speeding forward. The rest had halted or were fleeing.

In a smooth gesture Nate drew his left flintlock, seized the reins in the same hand that held the Hawken, and came to an abrupt stop within a dozen feet of the man in black, who had slumped over in apparent exhaustion, head touching the ground. He vaulted from the saddle, faced the charging predators, and sighted on the foremost. The flintlock spat flame and smoke. Hit squarely between the eyes, the wolf was flipped onto its back by the impact.

The remainder had had enough. As one they veered sharply to the left and sped to the northwest.

Nate watched them go, jamming the spent flintlock under his belt so he could draw the second one. Only when he was convinced they were actually leaving did he step to the man's side and squat. "You're safe now. How bad off are you?"

Grunting, the man lifted his head and mustered a grin. He was in his late twenties or early thirties and wore his dark brown hair down to his shoulders. His eyes, also brown, conveyed his gratitude at being saved. "Thank you, brother," he said softly. "I was a goner if you hadn't come along."

Brother? Nate put a hand on the man's thin shoulder. "Can you stand? Where are you hurt?"

"I fell yesterday on some rocks but I'm not seriously injured," the man said, pushing off the ground with his left hand so he could stand. As he straightened, swaying from the effort, he revealed a book clutched in his right fist.

Nate saw the title as he rose. *The Holy Bible*. He figured the man must be extremely religious to have held onto the Scriptures when it would have been smarter to toss the bible aside in order to run faster.

"My name is John Burke. I apologize for any trouble I've put you to," the man said, smiling.

"How did you come to be in this fix?"

"My horse and pack animals were stolen by Indians three days ago and I haven't eaten or had a drop of water since." Burke indicated his right leg where the fabric had been torn and his skin split open. "After I fell, I bled for quite a while. The wolves must have picked up the scent."

Nate nodded in agreement and stuck the flintlock under his belt to free his hands for loading the Hawken. "I'm Nate King. If you're agreeable, I'll take you to a Shoshone village not very far from here."

"Shoshones? Are they friendly?"

"There are none friendlier. I've lived among them off and on for nine years. My wife is Shoshone."

"Oh," Burke said, and absently began chewing on his lower lip, evidently in deep thought. He did not appear pleased at the prospect.

Nate was about to inquire into the reason Burke had been traveling across the prairie all alone when a low growl from directly behind him chilled his blood and gave him goose flesh. He whirled in alarm. There, not six feet away, was the enormous gray wolf he had shot in the side, upright and crouching to spring.

Chapter Two

Living in the raw wild changed a man. He learned to rely on his natural instincts if he wanted to survive. Where a comfortable city life often dulled a man's senses and made him physically flabby, the wilderness tempered him like a forge tempered a steel blade, firming his muscles until they were rock hard and honing his reflexes until they were as sharp as the wild beasts he frequently confronted.

So it was that at the very moment Nate laid eyes on the crouching wolf, he released the Hawken and threw himself to the right while clawing at the flintlock he had just wedged under his belt. The wolf was incredibly quick, springing as his hand closed on the gun, and Nate realized in a flash that he would be unable to get off a shot before the beast was on him. In a twinkling he shifted his hand to his knife, and was drawing the weapon when the wolf slammed into him.

Nate was bowled over, landing on his back with the snarling wolf on top of his chest. Snapping jaws narrowly missed his face. He thrust a forearm under the wolf's jaw to keep it from biting again while simultaneously thrusting the butcher knife into the animal's ribs. Again he stabbed, trying to pierce the heart, but he only succeeded in arousing the wolf to a frenzied pitch of feral wrath. Razor teeth bit into his wrist, ripping the skin, and he felt the clammy sensation of blood flowing down his arm. Claws tore at the front of his buckskin shirt. In desperation Nate bunched both shoulders and heaved, hoping to fling the beast from him. But the wolf clung to his wrist, its teeth grinding deeper.

Twisting, Nate drove the blade into the wolf's throat. The animal recoiled, its teeth slipping from his arm. With a lunge Nate rose to his knees, the knife held close to his chest, ready to thrust again. Out of the corner of his eye he saw John Burke a yard away, motionless, making no move to come to his aid.

The wolf growled, blood spraying from the hole in its neck, and jumped.

Nate rose, meeting the beast halfway, his blade arcing into the base of the wolf's throat once more, impaling it to the hilt. He wrenched the knife free, then slid to the left, giving himself room to maneuver. As he did he grabbed his tomahawk, and when the wolf leaped yet again he employed both weapons at once, ramming the knife into the animal's neck and slamming the tomahawk down on the top of the wolf's skull.

Thudding to the ground, its head split open to expose its brains, a crimson geyser erupting from its throat wounds, the wolf thrashed violently and snapped at the empty air. Gradually its limbs quieted and its head slumped limply; then the beast gasped and expired.

Nate half expected it to rise again. If there was a single trait many kinds of animals shared, it was an abiding tenacity that would cling to life at all costs. This wolf had been a prime example. Mortally wounded, it had attacked again and again. As the trappers often said about the mighty grizzly bear, the wolf had been hard to die.

He wiped the back of his sleeve across his sweating brow and struggled to calm his pounding heart. A glance at his forearm showed the bite marks weren't as deep as he had feared. Another glance, at John Burke, demonstrated his anger. "Thanks for the help," he said bitterly.

"I'm sorry, brother, but there was nothing I could do."

"You could have kicked it. You could have beaten it with your bible. Hell, you could have done anything but just stand there like a bump on a log," Nate told him.

Burke's features drooped in regret. "No, I could not. It is against my beliefs to do harm to any of God's creatures."

"Even when one of those creatures is trying to tear you apart?"

John Burke nodded and gazed into Nate's eyes. "I should explain. I'm *Reverend* John Burke, a missionary."

"You don't say," Nate said to cover his embarrassment. In all his years in the wild he had only run into two other men of the cloth, both missionaries on their way to the Oregon country. They had stopped at the site of the last Rendezvous and mingled with the trappers and Indians on hand for the annual festivities. Their presence had created quite a stir. Ministers and priests were as rare as hen's teeth beyond the established frontier.

"I've come all the way from Rhode Island," Burke was saying. "The Lord wants me to minister to the heathens, to show them the light, to lead them to an understanding of our Savior, Jesus Christ."

"That's a pretty tall order," Nate commented. "Most of the Indians I know are happy with the religion they have."

"Indians have religion?" Burke responded skeptically. "I was under the impression they practice barbaric rites of self-torture under the guise of Nature worship."

"Do you know any Indians personally?"

"No, but I've talked to many men who have contacted the heathens and I know . . ." Burke broke off, touching a palm to his brow as he unexpectedly tottered. "Oh, my! I'm afraid everything is catching up with me."

"Are you faint?"

"I feel dizzy. So very dizzy," the reverend said. His eyelids fluttered and he groaned. Then, without warning, he pitched forward.

Nate caught Burke in his arms before the man could strike the earth. His wrist flared with pain, and he grimaced as he gently lowered Burke onto his back. Stepping to the stallion, he removed his bedroll and unfolded the blanket he used at night. Inside was a spare shirt courtesy of Winona, an extra ammo pouch, and an extra set of moccasins. Because his line of work entailed repeatedly wading into frigid streams to lay traps and collect dead beaver, those moccasins frequently came in handy when the pair he normally wore became soaked. Using his knife, he cut off a strip from the hem of his spare shirt, then washed his wrist with water from his water skin before bandaging the bite marks as best he could. He did a crude job, but he wasn't worried about infection setting in. By nightfall he would be back at the village where Winona would doctor him with herbal medicines that were every bit as effective as anything white physicians relied on. In many instances the herbs were even better.

Replacing the bedroll, he carried the water skin to Burke and knelt. The man was unconscious, breathing regularly, the bible still clasped in his right hand. He tilted Burke's head and carefully let the cool water trickle between the reverend's parted lips. After a bit Burke sputtered, coughed, and opened his eyes.

"I passed out, didn't I?"

"Yes," Nate confirmed, capping the bag.

"I'm sorry to be such a bother. Give me a little food

and I'll be as fit as a fiddle.''

"Quit apologizing," Nate said, standing and securing the water skin to the saddle. "You're holding up fine considering all you've been through." He tapped the sack that contained his grub. "I can offer you a few strips of fresh jerked venison. They'll have to tide you over until we reach the village. Trying to eat too much right now would only make you sick to your stomach."

"I see. Jerky it is then."

Nate selected an especially thick piece. "My wife smoked the meat herself," he said as he handed the salted venison over. "I can guarantee you've never tasted more delicious jerky anywhere."

Burke cocked his head and regarded Nate with a puzzled expression. "You sound very proud of her."

"I am."

"You *like* being married to a squaw?"

Anger made Nate scowl. Had another trapper asked such an insulting question, he would have torn into the offender with his fists flying. But the minister's voice betrayed no hint of sarcasm, his features no trace of effrontery. Nate suppressed his resentment and replied in a calm tone. "Yes, I do, Reverend. Winona is a lovely woman." He paused. "And I'll thank you to never, ever refer to her as a *squaw* again. It's not the most flattering of terms."

"Oh," Burke said. "I didn't realize. Folks back East call Indian women squaws all the time."

"And do they ever mean it as a compliment?"

The thin man pondered for several seconds. "No, I suppose they don't. Most of our kind don't hold the red race in very high regard, which is to be expected when a superior culture clashes with an inferior one."

"You sound like President Jackson," Nate said testily. Andrew Jackson, or Old Hickory as he was commonly called, was in his second term. When Jackson first ran for the office, he'd publicly declared his belief that Indians were an inferior race, and asserted the U.S. government had an obligation to reorganize them as it saw fit.

"I take it you disagree with his policies?" Burke asked.

"If you knew the Indian people as well as I do, you'd disagree with him too," Nate declared, and extended a hand. "Now why don't we get you on my horse? The sooner we get started, the sooner I'll have you resting and well fed in my lodge."

John Burke allowed himself to be helped to his feet and given a boost onto Pegasus. He sagged, nearly pitched off, and gripped the saddle to brace himself.

"Can you manage?" Nate asked.

"The Lord will sustain me."

Nate pointed at the bible. "Let me put that in my sack for the time being."

"No."

"You can't ride well using just one hand."

"I'll be all right," Burke insisted, and wagged the holy book. "This is the only bible I have left. The rest were stolen by the same band of heathens who took my horses. I'll need this when I begin my ministry, and I'm not letting it out of my sight."

Nate thought the man was being foolish, but dropped the matter. He began reloading his guns. As he worked he scoured the plain for the wolf pack, but saw no sign of them. "Did you get a look at the Indians who stole your animals and provisions?"

"A glimpse was all," Burke said. He bit off a small piece of jerky and chewed slowly. "I had made camp in a stand of trees and gone off a ways from my fire to heed Nature's call. The next thing I knew my horses were acting up, so I ran back in time to see five redskins escaping to the northeast with all my worldly possessions." He sadly shook his head. "I didn't mind losing my food and blankets half as much as I did the ten bibles I brought along.

I intended to present them to savages who would accept Jesus as their Savior.''

Though engrossed in pouring the proper amount of black powder down the barrel of his Hawken, Nate paused and glanced up. "You have your work cut out for you, Reverend Burke. Most Indians I know think the white man's religion is downright strange."

Burke straightened. "I'll show them otherwise, Mr. King. I'll open their eyes to the truth. I have to. God commanded me to do so in a dream."

Nate didn't quite know what to say to that. He busied himself reloading the flintlock, then wiped his knife and tomahawk on one of the dead wolves to remove the blood and gore. Once all his weapons except the rifle were snug under his belt, he shouldered the Hawken, took hold of the reins, and hiked westward.

For the next half an hour they traveled in silence. Burke ate three strips of venison and greedily drank from the water skin between each piece.

Shortly thereafter, tree-covered foothills appeared. Beyond them reared snowcapped peaks glistening bright in the golden sunlight.

"Are those the Rockies?" Burke asked in awe.

Nate nodded, recalling the very first time he beheld a section of the chain of magnificent rocky ramparts that extended from just north of Santa Fe all the way up into Canada. The stirring sight of those rugged summits towering thousands and thousands of feet into the azure sky had thrilled him to his core. Right then and there he had decided to stay, although he hadn't quite realized the fact at the time. The Rockies held an allure that attracted his soul like a magnet attracted iron. In his estimation they were the pinnacle of creation, so sublimely beautiful as to defy description. "You should see the range down near where I live," he commented. "The peaks are even higher than these."

"You don't live with the Shoshones?"

"We have a cabin about a two-week ride to the south, near Long's Peak," Nate disclosed, referring to an exceptionally high mountain named after Major Stephen Long, who had been searching for the source of the Platte River back in 1820 when he spied the peak that would subsequently bear his name. In the 17 years since then, only a score or so of white men had also seen the mountain, which was well off the beaten path, being far north of the Santa Fe Trail and far south of the prime beaver territory regularly crisscrossed by the trappers. "At least once a year we visit's my wife's people and spend a month or so with them."

"Could it have been Shoshones who stole my belongings?"

"No."

"How can you be so certain?"

"Two reasons. First, the Shoshones don't go in for stealing from whites like some of the tribes do. Second, if you were three days from here when it happened, you were in Cheyenne and Sioux country. If I had to make a wager, I'd bet it was a band from one or the other that hit you."

"Could it have been the Blackfeet?"

Nate looked at the minister. "You know about them?"

An enigmatic smile curled Burke's lips. "I've heard a little."

"Then you must know the Blackfeet are the most bloodthirsty devils alive. They're constantly raiding other tribes. And they hate whites. If a war party of Blackfeet had found your camp, you'd be minus your hide right about now."

Burke touched a hand to his lower back and arched his spine to relieve a cramp. "I suppose I'll never know for sure which tribe was responsible." He swiveled and gazed out over the prairie. "Then again, perhaps I will."

"What do you mean?"

The minister pointed to the east. "If I'm not mistaken, here comes the same band that raided my camp."

Nate spun in alarm, leveling the Hawken as he turned. Not five hundred yards away were five warriors riding straight toward them.

Chapter Three

Nate stepped between Pegasus and the oncoming braves, his thumb on the Hawken's hammer, and adopted a casual air. Indian men admired courage above all else. If he displayed any fear, the band might see fit to try and take his stallion. He could tell by the style in which they wore their braided hair, the fashion of their buckskin leggings, and the painted symbols on their mounts that they were indeed Cheyennes. One was leading a saddled horse and a pair of packhorses.

"Those are my animals," the minister declared.

"I figured as much," Nate said, forcing a smile. The warriors had not made any threatening gestures; their bows were slung over their shoulders, their knifes in their sheaths. Only one man held a lance, the tip pointed at the ground to show his intentions were friendly. Nate waited until the five were 20 feet away before tucking the Hawken under his right hand and using sign language to greet them. They promptly reined up. A stocky warrior bearing a scar on his right cheek kneed his pony forward a few paces and returned the greeting.

"I am Speckled Snake of the Cheyenne," the man went on. "We come in peace, white man."

Nate kept his eyes on the others as he lifted his hands. "I am Grizzly Killer," he responded, using the Indian name bestowed on him years ago by a noted Cheyenne warrior known as White Eagle. Now the Shoshones, Nez Percé, Crows, and Flatheads all called him by that name.

Murmuring broke out among the warriors. Speckled Snake cocked his head and studied Nate from head to toe. "You are known to me. They say you kill grizzlies as other men kill rabbits. They say you have counted many coup on your enemies."

"What they say is true," Nate acknowledged. He wasn't boasting so much as making it plain to the five warriors that he was a man to be reckoned with, and that if they started trouble they could count on a fight.

"They say you have even killed many Blackfeet."

"I have," Nate signed. In truth, he couldn't remember the exact number. But the Blackfeet had been a persistent thorn in his side ever since he came to the Rockies, There had been the time a war party attacked his wife's people, and the time another band kidnapped one of his best friends. Not quite a year ago he had tangled with them again when they raided the Nez Percé. It was rumored the Blackfeet wanted his scalp more than that of any other white man, which was why he made a point of going nowhere near their territory.

Speckled Snake nodded at the minister. "Is this man a friend of yours?"

"He is," Nate replied, deliberately keeping his answers short in case the Cheyennes were trying to deceive him and made a play for their weapons.

"We did not know that," Speckled Snake signed. He twisted to indicate the three spare horses. "These are his.

He is welcome to have them back.''

"I thank you."

The stocky warrior motioned, and the Cheyenne holding the lead brought the horses forward, then wheeled and moved back beside his companions.

John Burke cleared his throat. "I don't understand, King. Why are they giving my animals back? What did you do? Threaten to shoot them?"

"No. They're returning the horses of their own free will."

"I can't believe that. Everyone knows Indians are inveterate thieves."

Speckled Snake had been listening to the exchange with interest. He pointed at the reverend and asked in sign, "What did he say?"

"He also thanks you for giving his animals back," Nate lied in the interest of keeping the peace. If he translated the minister's exact words, the Cheyennes would be insulted. And unlike whites, Indian men never allowed an insult to go unchallenged.

"Does he want to know why we followed him?"

"He is curious," Nate signed, only because he was intensely curious himself. By all rights the five warriors should be back at their village, reveling in their spoils. It was unheard of for a raiding party to return the goods they took. The only reason he could think of for why the Cheyennes trailed Burke was to finish him off and take whatever the reverend had on him.

The stocky warrior squared his shoulders. "We wanted to find out why he does not carry any weapons."

Nate held his right hand at shoulder height, his palm outward, his fingers and thumb pointed upwards and slightly separated, and turned the hand by wrist action three times in succession. The gesture was an all-purpose sign that stood not only for "what," but also "why," "when," and "where," depending on the context in which it was used. In this instance he was asking Speckled Snake to repeat himself since he felt he might have misunderstood.

"The skinny white does not carry weapons," the Cheyenne signed, and elaborated. "There were no guns or knives on his animals. All we found was a small ax for chopping wood." He stared at Burke. "We had watched him for a whole day before we took his horses, so we knew he did not carry a weapon on his person. We believed we would find them in his packs, but we were wrong."

Nate pursed his lips. The warriors must have been terribly disappointed, since most would give their right arm to own a white man's rifle. Ordinarily, Indians received only inferior trade guns known as fusees. A warrior who owned a genuine Hawken or other fine rifle was highly esteemed. Among the Blackfeet, any warrior who took an enemy's rifle received the highest honors. In fact, the Blackfoot word for war honor was *namachkani*, which literally meant "a gun taken."

"Who is this man who is so brave he travels without any means of protecting himself?" Speckled Snake signed earnestly.

Nate almost grinned at the confused look on the Cheyenne's bronzed face. Some of the others appeared equally perplexed. He could readily appreciate why they were baffled since it was unheard of for a warrior to go about unarmed. Even in their villages they seldom strayed far from their bows and lances since an enemy war party might strike at any time. And they undoubtedly knew that white men were always armed to the teeth with flintlocks, rifles, knives, and tomahawks.

"What's happening?" John Burke inquired. "Why are they looking at me like that?"

"They're puzzled because you don't own any weapons."

"How extraordinary. Well, inform them I'm a man of

the cloth, that it is against my religious convictions to harm another human being, even simple savages such as themselves.''

Speckled Snake motioned. ''What are his words?''

Again Nate hedged. ''The reason he does not carry weapons is because he has devoted his life to the Great Medicine,'' he signed, using the term that stood for God in most Indian tongues. The literal translation of ''medicine'' was ''mysterious'' or ''unknown.'' So when someone mentioned the Great Medicine, they were referring to the Great Mystery. Some of the mountain men claimed the expression should be translated as the Great Spirit, but ''medicine'' was the word most used by the Indians themselves.

The Cheyenne's surprise was transparent. ''The skinny one is a medicine man?''

''Yes,'' Nate replied, and in a sense he was right. Medicine men were tribal clergymen and doctors combined, leading spirit ceremonies when the occasion demanded and healing illnesses that arose. In some tribes they were more like clergymen than doctors, while in other tribes the reverse was true. Many whites made light of the Indian holy men, but from his own experiences Nate knew they were often wise, caring, and dedicated to the welfare of their people. In all tribes the medicine men were as highly esteemed as the chiefs, perhaps more so. By telling these Cheyennes that Burke was a medicine man, he was insuring they would hold the reverend in the highest regard and never bother him again.

Turning, Speckled Snake began an animated conversation with his fellow warriors. At length he faced Nate and signed, ''What is his name?''

Nate had to think before responding. There were no sign gestures for proper names in the English language, which was why trappers who chose to live among the Indians always took an Indian name and used it in all their dealings with the various tribes. He must make one up for Burke, and it should be something appropriate. "Medicine Teacher," he answered, which sparked a new round of discussion.

"Tell him we did not know he was a medicine man when we took his horses," Speckled Snake said in due course. "Had we known, we would never have bothered him." He lowered his hands briefly. "Ask Medicine Teacher if he is angry with us. We do not want him to put bad medicine on our heads for our mistake."

John Burke leaned toward Nate. "What the dickens is this heathen babbling about now?"

"They're afraid you'll put a curse on them."

"By George, I should!" Burke bellowed, jabbing a finger at Speckled Snake. "I should call down the wrath of the Lord on you and your pathetic, ignorant people for what you've done to me! But I won't. And do you know why?" He glowered at the five Cheyennes, then quoted from Scripture. "The Lord is my defense, and my God is the rock of my refuge. And he shall bring upon them their own iniquity, and shall cut them off in their own wickedness. Yea, the Lord our God shall cut them off." Smiling fiercely, Burke straightened. "Your own wickedness will be your undoing, savages. I need not lift a finger against you."

The fiery outburst had agitated the Cheyennes, who began whispering among themselves.

"What did Medicine Teacher say?" Speckled Snake inquired. "He sounds displeased."

Nate hesitated, simmering with indignation. Here he was, trying his best to convince these warriors that Burke and he were as friendly as could be, and the good reverend was doing his damnedest to stir them up. Already one of the warriors was fingering the hilt of his knife. If Burke wasn't careful, he'd get the Cheyennes downright mad. And medicine man or not, they wouldn't stand still for being insulted. He smiled to reassure them, then signed, "Medicine Teacher is angry, but not at you. He is angry at himself because his medicine failed him. He ate something he should not have eaten, and that is why the Great Medicine did not keep his horses and possessions safe."

"I understand," Speckled Snake said gravely.

It paid to be familiar with Indian customs, Nate reflected. Among many tribes it was customary for young warriors to go on vision quests to obtain spiritual power. By going off by themselves and fasting until an extraordinary dream, or vision, presented itself, they hoped to gain supernatural powers that would protect them in battle. A warrior might see a red hawk in a dream, for instance, and paint it on his shield to ward off enemy arrows. But with their new power usually came taboos. In order for the hawk shield to be effective, the warrior might have to refrain from eating the brains of a buffalo or from letting a menstruating woman come near it. The taboos were endless and varied, depending on how the warriors interpreted their dreams.

In the same vein, medicine men often went on vision quests to obtain healing powers or other abilities. And like the warriors, they had to stick to certain rules or their powers would be useless.

"We will leave you in peace," Speckled Snake now signed. "And we will tell our people of this meeting so they may learn that white men do know of the Great Medicine. There are some who believe all whites are dead inside, like rotten trees that can never bear ripe fruit, and know nothing of spirit matters."

Nate made the signs for "Go in peace." He sighed in relief as the five Cheyennes galloped off to the northeast without looking back, and felt the tension drain from his body. "That was close," he remarked.

"Why? Did those devils threaten to harm us?"

"No, but if you had opened your mouth one more time they just might have."

"What is that supposed to mean?"

Nate pivoted. "It means, Reverend, you have a lot to learn if you want to survive out here. Indians will not abide insults. You can't treat them like you would your congregation back in the States."

"I'll speak to them as the spirit of the Lord moves me," Burke said gruffly. "If they're offended, so be it."

"If they're offended, they might just turn you into a pincushion."

Burke smiled. "I'm prepared to be a martyr if that's what it takes to get these primitives to see the light."

"Suit yourself," Nate said with a shrug. Suddenly he was sorry he had ever run into the man. There was no reasoning with someone like him, and the way Burke was going it wouldn't be long before he got his wish and wound up scalped. Nate didn't want to be around when it happened. He would probably lose his life trying to save Burke's, and he had a wife and son to think of, "Reckon you're fit enough to ride your own horse?" he asked.

"I believe I can, yes."

"Then let's go. I want to reach the Shoshone village before nightfall," Nate said. He stood to one side as the minister dismounted, then climbed on Pegasus. "If you have no objections, I'll handle your pack animals."

"Very well," Burke said, stepping to his bay and climbing slowly up. He patted the animal's neck. "I knew the Lord would provide for me. See how He watches over his children?"

Nate grabbed the lead rope and clucked the stallion into a trot. For over an hour they rode steadily westward until they reached the base of the foothills, where he drew rein to give the stallion a short breather before forging onward. To the north, well out of rifle range, was a small herd of black-tailed deer. To the south a bald eagle circled far above the gently waving prairie grass. He inhaled deeply, enjoying the fragrance of the nearby pines.

Burke had said nothing the whole time, but he now saw fit to speak. "I appreciate what you did for me back there, Brother King. You're quite a hand at dealing with Indians, aren't you?"

"I should be after living among them for so long," Nate replied, glancing at the reverend just as Burke's eyes became the size of saucers and his mouth drooped open in astonishment. Swiveling, Nate gazed in the same direction and saw an enormous grizzly bear emerging from the forest.

Chapter Four

Of all the animals in the wilderness, grizzlies were the most feared by whites and Indians alike. Tremendous in size, with extremely wide heads, massive shoulders, and prominent humps that set them apart from their black cousins, grizzlies were the masters of their domain. Even panthers and wolverines gave them a wide birth. Sometimes rising to over eight feet in height when they stood on their hind legs, grizzlies were endowed with terrible claws over four inches long. A single swipe could disembowel a grown moose or decapitate a man.

Nate felt his mouth go dry as the grizzly started out across the plain, its huge head swinging ponderously from side to side, lumbering clumsily along, giving no hint of the startling speed of which a grown bear was capable. It was 50 yards away and as yet had not noticed them. If they didn't move it might keep on going. Grizzlies had notoriously poor sight. Their sense of smell, however, was exceptional. Hopefully the wind wouldn't carry their scent to it.

The monster abruptly halted and sniffed.

"What do we do?" Burke whispered.

"Don't move and don't talk," Nate advised. He saw the bear look toward them and gulped. Burke's bay was swishing its tail. The grizzly was bound to notice. Sure enough, a second later the beast took a heavy stride in their direction while continuing to test the wind.

"The Lord preserve us!" Burke breathed.

"When I tell you to, ride like you've never ridden before," Nate directed. "Head westward and don't look back."

"What about you?"

"I'll try and get the bear to chase me. After I lose it, I'll fire shots so you can find me again."

"What if it catches you?"

"My wife's name is Winona. Follow the setting sun until you come to a lake. The Shoshone village is on the south side. Let her know what happened."

"Your sacrifice won't be necessary," Burke declared. "I have a better idea."

"Such as?" Nate asked, and was flabbergasted when the minister unexpectedly turned his horse toward the bear, held his bible aloft, and shouted at the top of his lungs.

"Begone, foul beast! In the name of Our Lord Jesus I command you to leave us be!"

The grizzly uttered a fearful roar and charged.

"Damn!" Nate snapped, and swiftly gave the bay's rump a solid smack that sent the horse racing into the trees with Reverend Burke clinging to the saddle for dear life. Clutching the rope lead, Nate angled to the northwest and waved the Hawken to attract the bear. "This way!" he yelled. "Come after me, you mangy varmint!"

Loping faster than a man could run, the grizzly bore down on the horses.

In a twinkling Nate was wending among fir and spruce trees, a wall of branches momentarily screening him from the attacking monster. Ordinarily Pegasus could handily outdistance one of the giant bruins, but now the pack animals were slowing the stallion down. Burdened as they were with more supplies than was practical for a horse to carry, the pair was doing their best but still going nowhere near fast enough to escape the pursuing behemoth.

A branch plucked at Nate's beaver hat as he skirted a pine and crossed a narrow clearing. To his rear arose the loud crackle of underbrush, telling him the grizzly had entered the trees. His only hope was to stay ahead of the beast for the next two or three hundred yards. Provided he succeeded, the grizzly would tire and give up the chase. If not . . .

The forest was a blur. Nate had to constantly change direction to avoid trunks, logs, and boulders. Once the tip of a limb snagged his chin but his beard spared him from being cut. The ground sloped uphill, so he bore to the right until he came to a dry wash between two hills. The level stretch enabled him to urge the horses to go even faster.

At the west end of the wash, where it broadened out into a lush valley, he galloped madly toward a stand of aspen, the nearest available cover. A quick glance showed the grizzly just bursting from the woods.

Did he dare risk a shot?

No, he decided, because the odds of killing a grizzly with a single ball were slim. No less a personage than the famous Meriwether Lewis, of Lewis and Clark fame, had first chronicled the difficulty of slaying grizzlies in the journal he kept on his trek to the Pacific Ocean in 1805. When the men of the expedition initially encountered the gigantic brutes, they treated the grizzlies much as they would black bears from the States. But the first bear they shot for its meat and oil took ten balls before it dropped—

five through the lungs. Another grizzly was shot eight times as it tried to chase down and slay some of the members of the expedition. From then on Lewis and Clark treated the monsters with cautious respect.

Nate reached the aspens and darted into them. The grizzly was still in heated pursuit, rumbling continuously deep in its immense chest. Nate battered branches aside with the Hawken as he made for a field beyond the stand. The foremost pack animal bumped into a tree and stopped, catching him unawares, and he was nearly pulled from the saddle. With a frantic jerk on the rope he got the horse moving again.

Puffing noisily as its great feet struck the ground in steady cadence, the bear barreled onward.

Past the aspens Nate gave the stallion its head. He was strongly tempted to let go of the lead so he could escape, but he held on, his arm straining almost beyond endurance. The grizzly crashed into the stand and Nate swore the ground shook. The bear roared in frustration, the tightly spaced trunks slowing it down as he had planned.

More forest lay 60 yards ahead. To the right of the woods was a boulder-strewn hill. He made for the woodland, and was halfway there when over the top of the hill rode two warriors who promptly stopped on spying him. There was no time to determine if they were friendly or not. Already the grizzly had exited the stand and resumed the chase with renewed vigor.

Nate was beginning to think he would have no choice but to halt and fire. He could see the pair of warriors moving down the slope to intercept him. Perhaps they were hostiles intent on picking him off while he was preoccupied. One of them held a bow, and in the hands of a skilled warrior an arrow could slay a foe from a hundred yards off. He heard the warriors commence whooping and hollering and slowed just enough for a good look.

They were Shoshones.

Elated, he saw them angling toward the bear, not toward him. An instant later he recognized the duo as Drags the Rope and Beaver Tail. The former he had met on the very day he'd met Winona, and he was a close friend. Beaver Tail was a younger man barely out of his teens who had yet to count coup on a foe.

What in the world were they doing? Nate wondered. Both were beaming and lashing their war ponies with their leather quirts, clearly trying to reach the grizzly before it could overtake him. He saw Drags the Rope nock an arrow to his bowstring and Beaver Tail heft a lance. With a start he realized they were going to try and slay the monster.

Nate looked over his right shoulder to discover the bear had heard their clamor, spied them, and halted. Nate was in the clear. All he had to do was keep on going and there was no way the grizzly could harm him. The Shoshones would keep it occupied, although in the process both of them might lose their lives. Hauling on the reins, he jumped down and hastily tied the lead rope to a bush, then remounted and raced back.

Already the warriors were clear of the hill and sweeping toward the waiting bear. The monster seemed to sense their intent. It growled and swung a stupendous paw as if inviting them to try their best.

Drags the Rope raised his bow, sighted, and let the shaft fly when 40 feet from the grizzly. Streaking true to his aim, the arrow sliced into the bear's shoulder below the neck, sinking in all the way to the eagle feather fletching.

The grizzly vented a roar of rage and twisted its head to snap at the protruding feathers. Its jaws closed shy of the shaft. Thwarted, growling ferociously, it glowered at the onrushing Shoshones, then charged.

The warriors continued to close. Riding expertly, horse and rider as one, Drags the Rope cut to the right and sent a second arrow into the slavering brute. The bear slanted toward him, covering the ground with astounding speed.

It appeared certain the grizzly would be on him in seconds.

Beaver Tail whooped and galloped straight at the monster. He whipped his arm overhead, straightened, and tensed to hurl his lance into the bear's side. But the beast heard the pounding of his mount's hoofs. It whirled to face him, its jaws wide, its glistening teeth exposed.

Swerve aside! Nate wanted to shout. Evidently the young warrior had no intention of doing so. He saw Beaver Tail grin, saw the lance leap from the Shoshone's hand and strike the grizzly in the chest, then watched in horror as the young warrior tried to turn his horse too late. The bear, ignoring the lance imbedded in its body, took two quick steps and arced its right forepaw into the horse's head.

Blood sprayed from the war pony's crushed skull as the animal staggered, then toppled, hitting the ground on its right side. At the last instant Beaver Tail tried to leap to safety but the horse came down on his leg, pinning him. He drew a knife and twisted to defend himself from the approaching bear.

The grizzly halted and cocked its head regarding the young warrior intently. It placed a front leg on the dead war pony and started to step over the horse to get at Beaver Tail.

Yipping like a coyote, Drags the Rope galloped in close and unleashed a shaft into the monster's neck. The bear spun and roared, then sprang at Drags the Rope's mount, its paw flashing. The horse was struck on the flank, lost its balance, and fell. Drags the Rope jumped clear, drawing another arrow from his quiver as he did. The grizzly, paying no attention to the war pony's wild thrashing as it tried to stand, moved toward him.

By then Nate was there, riding Indian fashion, using his legs to guide the stallion, the Hawken tucked tight against his right shoulder, the hammer cocked, his finger on the trigger. He came in at a gallop, and when only four

yards separated Pegasus from the growling monster he
fired, aiming at a point in front of the bear's right ear.
The grizzly whirled and tried to rip open Pegasus with its
great claws, but at a jerk of the reins and a jab of Nate's
heels the stallion bounded aside.

Roaring hideously, the bear gave chase, traveling a
dozen yards before it abruptly stopped and began shaking
its huge head as if perplexed. It took a few lumbering
steps, then tottered unsteadily, swiped a forepaw at the air
a few times, and collapsed, sinking slowly to the grass
with its front legs outstretched and its head coming to rest
between them.

Nate turned Pegasus and drew his left flintlock. The
bear was motionless but it might only be dazed. Of all the
creatures in the wilderness, grizzlies were the hardest to
kill. Single shots rarely sufficed, even in the head, because
their brains were protected by exceptionally thick skulls
plus two large muscles that covered the sides of the forehead and served to stop or deflect any shots. The common
phrase "hard to die" had in fact been coined by Meriwether Lewis in regards to the fierce beasts.

He drew within ten feet, aimed the flintlock, and fired.
The barrel belched smoke and lead, and he saw the ball
smack into the bear's head near the ear. The mighty animal
didn't budge. Nate cautiously rode nearer, tucking the
spent pistol under his belt and drawing the second flintlock
just in case. Sliding from the saddle, he warily stepped
up to the monster and touched the barrel to its brow.

The grizzly was still motionless, its eyes open but un-
blinking, pink drool flowing from its partially open mouth.
Blood trickled from the two holes in its head as well as
from the arrow and lance wounds. There could be no doubt
the bear was dead.

Nate exhaled and straightened. That had been too close
for comfort. Had the bear been a shade faster, it would
have knocked down Pegasus and had him at its mercy.

He heard footsteps and a hand clapped him on the back.

"Well done, Grizzly Killer! How many does this make now? Seven or eight?"

Turning, Nate looked at the smiling face of his close friend and smiled too, although not as broadly. By all rights he should be glad to be alive and savoring the thrill of triumph, but deep down he was bothered by the incident. He had never taken satisfaction in killing except when it was absolutely necessary, such as for food for his family, for clothing, or for beaver pelts to make a living. He wasn't one of those mountaineers who went around shooting animals for the sheer hell of it. And although he would kill in self-defense, he regretted having to take the life of a creature that was only acting according to its given nature. "Four," he said in perfect Shoshone. "I think this makes four."

"Wait until I tell everyone! No member of our tribe has ever killed so many brown bears and lived to talk about it. Touch the Clouds will be jealous."

"It was luck," Nate said. Touch the Clouds, the foremost Shoshone warrior, a giant of a man with muscles of steel, was another good friend. As with every Shoshone warrior, Touch the Clouds prided himself on the honors he earned on the battlefield or in fights with wild beasts, and had counted more coup than every Shoshone except their aged chief, Broken Paw. But the giant had only slain one grizzly, and even then had nearly lost his life when the bear tore his back open. It was well known among the tribe that Touch the Clouds was envious of Nate's widespread reputation as a slayer of grizzlies.

"You are too modest," Drags the Rope said, and nodded at the dead bear. "Only a man with courage and skill could have done as you did."

From off to the left came a shout. "If you are finished congratulating him, we have another visitor!" Beaver Tail interjected.

Nate glanced at the young warrior, who was still pinned under his horse, and saw Beaver Tail point to the south. Pivoting, he spied the reason for the Shoshone's concern. Standing at the edge of the trees was another bear.

Chapter Five

Nate's first thought was that the newcomer was the slain grizzly's mate. During courtship was the only time the bears traveled together; the rest of the time they were solitary in their habits. But he promptly realized this new bear was much smaller and darker than the monster he had shot. "It's a black bear," he said.

The animal watched them for a moment, then turned and hurried into the woods.

"It must have heard the roars and the shots and come to see what was happening," Drags the Rope guessed.

Nate nodded. Most animals were innately curious. Hopefully, Reverend John Burke had also heard the shots and would soon show up.

"I would go after it but I fear my horse is hurt," Drags the Rope said. "My family could use the meat."

"I'll share the meat from this brown bear with both of you," Nate proposed. "A third for each of us. What do you say?"

"We did nothing to earn it."

"You came to my aid when the bear was close behind me," Nate told him. "If not for you, I would be lying here and the beast would be feasting on my corpse." He motioned at Beaver Tail. "How about you? Does a third of the meat sound fair?"

"Very fair and generous," the young warrior replied. "And it is also fair that I help with the butchering, which I can not do while stuck under this stupid horse."

Drags the Rope laughed and nudged Nate. "Perhaps we should leave him there and divide the meat between ourselves. Any man foolish enough to let his own horse fall on him is not worth rescuing."

"And had I not put myself in a position where my horse could be slain, you would now be in the brown bear's belly," Beaver Tail countered indignantly.

Grinning, Nate walked over to help Drags the Rope free the younger Shoshone. When, years ago, he had first met the tribe, it had come as a considerable shock to him to learn that Indians possessed a wonderful sense of humor. Perhaps because of the grim image of Indians painted by the Eastern press, and the many insulting remarks about Indian behavior and intelligence made by the likes of President Jackson, he had always imagined Indians as stone-faced devils who never cracked a smile, let alone laughed. He had been delighted to learn otherwise, and he now thoroughly enjoyed the Shoshones' rough humor and horseplay.

Drags the Rope stood over the dead horse and scratched his chin. "What do you think, Grizzly Killer? Should we cut Beaver Tail's leg off at the knee to free him?"

"Just try," Beaver Tail retorted, wagging his knife, "and I will nail your tongue to the entrance of my lodge."

"Your father's lodge, you mean," Drags the Rope reminded him. "You have yet to take a wife, as I recall."

Nate saw the pinned warrior become beet-red. No warrior liked to be reminded of his youth and inexperience, so to prevent an argument Nate commented, "I would be willing to bet all the guns I own that when Beaver Tail does have his own lodge it will be one of the grandest in the village."

The young warrior blinked, then beamed and puffed out his chest. "Grizzly Killer is a wise man, just as everyone claims." He gave his dead war pony a whack with the flat of his hand. "Now would you please get this bag of skin and bones off me."

Stooping, Nate placed his hands under the animal's front shoulders while Drags the Rope imitated his example on the other side of Beaver Tail. "On the count of three," he said, and when Drags the Rope nodded, he began. "One. Two. Three." Together they lifted, each of them grunting and puffing, and succeeded in raising the top of the horse an inch or two, just high enough for Beaver Tail to slide his leg out with a supreme effort.

The young warrior pushed to his feet, then gave the horse a kick. "You failed me when I needed you the most. I will pick my next war pony more carefully."

Nate was inclined to blame Beaver Tail for the mount's death, but he said nothing. Indian men regarded their war horses almost as highly as they did their wives. Indeed, some warriors even took their war horses into their lodges at night if enemy raiding parties were believed to be in the vicinity of their village. And he knew of one man who regularly brought his steed inside on freezing cold winter nights and made his wife go sleep with her parents to make room for the horse. The attachment was understandable to one who understood the Indian way of life. Horses had become an essential part of Indian culture, as necessary for their survival as the limitless buffalo. Of all their animals, the highly trained and pampered war horse was the most highly esteemed because the warrior's life frequently depended on its performance. Quite an attachment developed between each warrior and his preferred stallion. When the horse failed in its duty, as Beaver Tail believed was the case here, it was as if a close personal friend had let the warrior down.

Drags the Rope was staring off at the pair of pack animals. "Are those yours, my friend?" he inquired.

"No," Nate answered, and briefly related his meeting with the minister.

"A white medicine man?" Drags the Rope remarked when Nate was done. "I have heard of such men but never met one. I look forward to talking with him." His eyes twinkled. "Perhaps he is not as strange as most whites."

Beaver Tail took the cue. "I too would like to meet this man. There must be one white somewhere who knows something about the Great Medicine."

"Persist in making fun of me and I will keep all the bear meat for myself," Nate threatened good-naturedly, and they all enjoyed a hearty laugh.

Next they examined Drags the Rope's chestnut. The bear's claws had left five slash marks, none of which were deeper than an inch. Otherwise, the horse was fine.

Nate took time to load his guns. He debated whether to fire more shots and decided to save the ammo, confident the minister would be able to find him.

Drawing their hunting knives, they set to work on the grizzly. After rolling the bear onto its side, they slit the hide on both hind legs, then cut a straight line from its tail to its chin. Nate slit the inside of the front legs. Exercising care, they peeled the pelt from the massive body, cutting ligaments and muscles where needed to part the hide from the carcass, always remembering to hold the edges of their knives toward the carcass and not the hide so as not to tear it. Their painstaking toil would eventually pay off, once the hide was cured, salted, soaked, fleshed, dehaired, and tanned by their women, in a heavy robe of excellent quality.

Nate stood and surveyed the surrounding forest. He had expected Reverend Burke to appear long before they were done removing the pelt, and he began to worry that in Burke's weakened state the minister might have suffered an accident. Bending down, he wiped his blade clean on the grass and looked at his companions. "Would the two of you watch those packhorses until I get back? I must go see what has happened to Medicine Teacher."

"We will not let anything happen to them," Drags the Rope promised.

Nate retrieved his Hawken, swung onto Pegasus, and headed southward. He was annoyed at himself for not firing more shots earlier to guide Burke along. The minister, after all, lacked Nate's wilderness savvy and might not be able to determine which direction the initial shots had come from.

He rode for a quarter of a mile, to the top of a high foothill, where he reined up to scour the countryside. The dense pines on the slopes and the thick vegetation in the valleys hindered his attempts to spot Burke. He did see a red hawk wheeling above timber to the southwest, a pair of ravens winging low over an adjacent valley, a lone bull elk grazing in a meadow, and far to the southeast, on the prairie, a small herd of buffalo. Squirrels chattered at him from the treetops and chipmunks scampered about seeking food. But there was no sign of another human being.

Drawing his left flintlock, he pointed the gun into the air and fired. While the echoes of the retort rolled among the hills and bounced off the steep sides of the mountains to the west, he reloaded the piece. For ten minutes or better he patiently waited, constantly scanning the open spaces, seeking the reverend.

His concern rising, Nate turned the stallion to the east and descended the hill. He pressed on until he reached the edge of the plain, then made for the spot where the grizzly had first appeared. Since gunshots weren't doing the trick, he would have to track Burke down. His years in the Rockies, where his very life and the lives of his loved ones often depended on his hunting skills, had turned him into a skilled tracker. He was confident he would find the minister before another hour went by.

Locating the point where they had separated proved easy enough. The hoofprints were clearly imbedded in the soil. He followed Burke's trail into the trees, able to determine by the length of the bay's stride and the depth of the tracks that Burke had been riding at a reckless speed. It wouldn't be surprising if he found the reverend sprawled out on the ground somewhere, his head caved in by a low limb.

Several hundred yards from the tree line the bay had slowed down. Burke, evidently, had finally gotten the animal under control. Inexplicably, the minister had also changed direction and was now traveling to the southwest. Puzzled, Nate trailed him. He had told Burke to go westward to find the Shoshone village. Why wasn't the man heeding his advice?

The forest gave way to a long, winding valley, a gently bubbling stream flowing down its center. The tracks led to the stream, where Burke had watered the bay, then proceeded up the valley in an erratic fashion. One second the trail would be close to the stream, the next veering off to a stand of trees or going close to a bordering hill. Then back to the stream again. It was as if Burke were taking a leisurely ride on a country estate back East, enjoying the sights as he went.

At last Nate spotted the bay, two hundred yards away, its head down as it cropped the sweet green grass in the shadow of a cluster of spruces. Where was Burke? His eyes narrowed as he spied a thin figure hunched low over the saddle, and with a flick of his feet he prodded the stallion into a trot.

The bay looked up at his approach, its ears pricked, its nostrils flaring. Burke was unconscious, a nasty welt on his forehead testifying to the cause.

"Whoa there, boy," Nate said softly to show the bay it had nothing to fear. "Remember me?" He leaned down to grasp its reins, then slid off Pegasus.

The reverend groaned.

Nate put a hand on Burke's shoulder. Other than the two-inch welt there were no other injuries that he could see. Evidently the minister had hit a tree limb after all, back in the forest, and the bay had taken it on itself to meander on a southwesterly course. "Reverend Burke?"

Uttering a short gasp, Burke sat bolt upright as his eyes snapped wide and he stared about him in confusion. "The trees!" he blurted. "The trees!" Then he noticed that the bay was standing still and saw Nate by his side. "You!" he said angrily. "I nearly lost my life when you gave my horse that whack. The contrary critter wouldn't stop no matter what I did."

"Would you rather have been caught by the grizzly?" Nate countered.

"No, of course not," Burke said, and gazed in all directions. "Where is the bear? And where the dickens am I? The last thing I remember is seeing a tree limb appear out of nowhere." He reached up and gingerly touched the welt. "Goodness. Now I know why my head is splitting."

Nate handed the reins up and mounted Pegasus. "The grizzly is dead. A couple of friends of mine showed up and gave me a hand when I needed it most."

"Fellow trappers?"

"Shoshones. They're watching your pack animals until we get back."

The minister frowned. "You're allowing a pair of heathens to guard my possessions? Isn't that like letting a fox guard the henhouse?"

"They won't steal anything, if that's what you're worried about."

"Unfortunately, Mr. King, I don't have your confidence

in these savages. At best they're like primitive children, and one should never place temptation before a child. They lack the self-discipline to behave properly."

"One of them is a close friend," Nate noted, annoyed by Burke's attitude. The man didn't even know Drags the Rope or Beaver Tail, yet he had no qualms about branding them as thieves, or worse. "I know him as well as I do myself. He's an honorable warrior, a decent human being."

Burke snorted. "I'm afraid you've been living among the heathens too long, brother. You see nobility in them where none exists. Tell me, is this friend of yours a Christian?"

"No, but—"

"Then I've made my point," Burke interrupted smugly. "Remember what the Good Book says about those who aren't Christian." He cleared his throat before quoting more Scripture. "Give not that which is holy unto the dogs, neither cast ye your pearls before swine, lest they trample them under their feet, and turn again and rend you."

Nate's lips compressed in a thin line. For Burke to accuse the Shoshones of being thieves had been bad enough. To call them dogs and pigs was more than he would tolerate. They were his adopted people, and he had come to know them as fine, intelligent, caring men and women who deserved as much respect as any white who ever lived. "For your information, Reverend, your belongings will be safer among the Shoshones than they would be in certain parts of New York City or St. Louis. As for them not being Christian, it's hardly their fault since no one has ever taught them our religion."

John Burke smiled. "Precisely. Which is why I'm here. God willing, I will lead the heathens to the true light. *I* will be the shining example that shows them the error of their savage ways. You just watch."

Chapter Six

The barking of a number of village dogs toward sunset drew the attention of three warriors conversing at the east edge of the encampment to the approaching party, and at their shouts Shoshones flocked from all directions to see who was coming.

Nate walked in the forefront, the Hawken in his left hand, leading Pegasus by the reins. His mood was a reflection of the storm clouds gathering to the west. Drags the Rope and Beaver Tail walked behind him. The three of them had secured the bear hide and as much meat as they could wrap inside it onto Pegasus, then packed more meat onto Drags the Rope's war horse. There had still been some left, and Nate had proposed tying it onto Burke's bay in order not to let it go to waste, but the minister had stubbornly refused to let his mount be used to haul a "miserable load of bloody meat."

The more Nate saw of the reverend, the less he liked the man. And he felt guilty for doing so. Burke was a

man of the cloth. Nate had been reared to always respect
the clergy, to believe they were special because they had
devoted their lives to God. Yet Burke made a mockery of
that devotion by flaunting it, and by regarding anyone who
didn't believe as he did as inferior.

Maybe, Nate reflected, he was being too critical. Burke
had been through hell out on the prairie, enduring hardships that would unsettle any man. Perhaps all it would
take was a hot meal and a good night's sleep to put him
in a better—friendlier—frame of mind.

There was much gesticulating and pointing among the
assembling Shoshones. Just arriving on the scene were a
pair Nate knew well. Chief Broken Paw was a wise old
man whose gray hairs and many wrinkles attested to the
fact he had earned his wisdom the hard way. Beside him
walked a giant to rival the Biblical Goliath, a warrior
almost seven feet tall who had one of the most fitting Indian
names Nate had ever heard. Touch the Clouds. He was
the son of a venerable warrior named Spotted Bull, who
in turn was the husband of Winona's aunt.

The chief and the giant moved a few feet in front of the
main crowd.

"What is this, Grizzly Killer?" Touch the Clouds
called. "You rode off to hunt buffalo and come back
walking your horse and bringing a stranger into our village?"

"I killed a brown bear instead of a buffalo," Nate responded, nodding at the hide on his stallion, and nearly
laughed aloud at the giant's stupefied expression.

"*Another* brown bear?" Chief Broken Paw said, smiling. "Keep this up and soon there will not be any left."

Nate shrugged and feigned a yawn. "It would serve
them right if they are wiped out. Any animal so easy to
kill will not last forever."

Touch the Clouds regained his composure and came

forward to inspect the pelt. "It seems to have been a very small bear," he commented

"How true," Drags the Rope said. "I only had to sit on my horse instead of stand on it to touch the bear's chin."

"You should have seen Grizzly Killer," Beaver Tail added, clearly amused at the giant's expense. "The bear had killed my brave horse and was about to do the same to Drags the Rope when Grizzly Killer rode right up to it. With no thought to his own danger, he shot it in the head."

"Grizzly Killer is a brave man," Touch the Clouds acknowledged in an odd tone.

By now the news had spread among the Shoshones and they were talking excitedly. Brown bears, as they called grizzlies, were the most formidable animals they knew, and they considered it a favorable omen, a sign of good medicine, when a tribal member killed one.

Nate's moment of glory was short-lived. He was about to relate the fight with the beast, as custom dictated, when John Burke rode up alongside him.

"What is all this jabbering about, brother? I'm on my last legs and these heathens are more interested in your flea-ridden hide."

Chief Broken Paw scrutinized the minister closely. "Who is this white man, Grizzly Killer? Why does he speak words that sting like bees?"

"His name is Medicine Teacher," Nate replied, and promptly wished he had thought to change the name to Rock Head. "I found him on the prairie. The Cheyennes had stolen his horses and left him to die."

The chief stared at Burke's bay and the two pack animals. "You got his horses back for him?"

"No. The Cheyennes returned them," Nate said, and detailed his encounter with the five warriors. The Shoshones listened attentively, some nodding, some whispering.

"This Medicine Teacher truly must be under the pro-

tection of the Everywhere Spirit,'' Chief Broken Paw remarked when Nate was done. ''It is unheard of for an
enemy to return stolen horses, especially the Cheyennes,
who are such expert horse thieves. It is the same as the
Blackfeet sparing a life, something that is never done.''
He smiled at Burke. ''I would be honored if this great
man would stay at my lodge during his time among our
people.''

''Who is this codger?'' the minister asked. ''And why
is he looking at me the way he is?''

Nate hoped his feelings toward Burke weren't showing
as he said to Broken Paw, ''Medicine Teacher is grateful
for your offer, but he has already agreed to stay at my
lodge. Rest assured we will come visit you as soon as he
is rested.''

''My lodge is always open to him.''

Neither Drags the Rope nor Beaver Tail made any comments, and Nate knew why. Although neither man spoke
English, they had been able to tell by Burke's attitude
earlier exactly what kind of man Burke was. They weren't
fooled by the name Nate had given him.

There was a commotion at the back of the crowd. Some
of the people parted to allow a raven-haired woman in a
beaded buckskin dress and a muscular boy of eight wearing
a typical Shoshone-style buckskin shirt and leggings to
pass through.

Nate momentarily forget all about Reverend Burke in
the heartfelt warm rush of seeing his loved ones again.
''Winona,'' he said softly, and took his wife into his arms,
savoring the minty scent of her hip-length tresses and the
feel of her soft but full body against his. Heedless of the
other Shoshones, he kissed her. Normally, members of
the tribe refrained from public displays of affection. Court-
ing couples often stood under blankets together in the
evenings, but by and large most of the men and women
were shy about showing their feelings toward one another

where all eyes could see. Most had long since become used to Nate's impulsive nature, laying the blame on his fiery white blood. A few of Winona's female friends had teased her about it, hinting that she must enjoy a lively blanket life of her own once the fire in their lodge was extinguished.

"Did I hear correctly, husband?" Winona asked in perfect English as she stepped back, her concerned brown eyes straying to the bear hide on Pegasus. "You had another run-in with a grizzly?"

"Afraid so," Nate replied. "And now you have a new robe."

The eight-year-old moved between them. "When will I get to kill a brown bear, Pa?"

Nate looked down into the hopeful face of his pride and joy, a spitting image of himself at that age but with the finer, more angular features of Winona's Shoshone ancestry mixed in. In keeping with the fact the boy had parents from two diverse cultures, two names had been bestowed on him at birth. Nate had picked Zachary, and both Winona and he had decided on Stalking Coyote for the child's Indian name. Except for a brief visit to St. Louis and the annual Rendezvous, the boy had never lived among white men. Now, at a distance, young Zach would pass for a full-blooded Shoshone. Only close up did it become apparent he was part white. "In due time, sprout," Nate answered. "A bird doesn't fly its first day in the nest. You're not quite old enough yet to tangle with a grizzly."

"Darn."

Reverend Burke coughed. "I take it this is your wife and son. How about introducing me, brother?"

"Certainly," Nate said, and proceeded to do so, noting how the minister gave Winona a cursory glance but studied Zach long and hard. He then explained that the minister would be staying at their lodge until fit to travel again.

"We will be honored to have you, Reverend," Winona graciously said.

"I must say, my dear, your English is excellent," Burke remarked.

"I've had an excellent teacher."

"Has your husband also taught you the Scriptures? Are you and your child Christians?"

"We do own a bible, Reverend. And Nate has told me much about the Lord God of your people. Still, there is much I do not understand."

Burke smiled. "Then it's good I have come. I'll be able to answer any questions you might have, and perhaps before I depart to minister to those I seek, I might have the pleasure of baptizing you and your son."

Nate glanced up, wondering what the minister meant by "those I seek," but before he could inquire the Shoshones clustered around them, some congratulating Nate on slaying the brown bear, some to get an account of the fight from Drags the Rope or Beaver Tail, and some to stare at the minister in frank curiosity. At length Nate was able to start toward his lodge. He let Zach lead Pegasus while he took the pack animals. Winona stayed close by his side.

Not all the Shoshones had congregated at the east side of the village. Small children scampered playfully about, frequently accompanied by frolicking dogs. Here and there women sat outdoors as they frequently did during the warmer months, either tanning hides, sewing clothes, repairing blankets, or doing any of the many domestic tasks they performed daily. Warriors were busy grooming their horses, sharpening knives, restringing bows, or doing other such activities regarded as fitting for a man. Among the Shoshones and other tribes there were clear-cut distinctions between the work performed by men and that performed by women, and it was exceedingly rare for a member of one sex to take up the crafts of the other.

Burke pointed at a circle of seated elderly warriors in

the middle of an argument. "What is that all about?" he inquired.

"They're gambling with dice made of buffalo bone," Nate disclosed, and saw the minister frown. "At the moment there is a dispute over a wager one of them made."

"I had no idea these heathens indulged in such wicked practices," Burke said, drawing a sharp glance from Winona. "Gambling is the earmark of the wicked and the playfellow of the lazy."

"My people have played at dice since the beginning of time," Winona responded. "It has not hurt us in any way."

"That's where you're wrong, I'm afraid. Gambling eats away at the soul like dry rot eats away the inside of trees. It's far better for men to turn to the Lord for their diversions than to take part in idle pursuits. Instead of rolling dice, those men would do better to spend their time giving thanks to God and praying for salvation."

More and more Nate was regretting his decision to bring Burke back to the village. It could only lead to trouble if the reverend didn't learn to keep quiet about matters that offended him. Nate had known many ministers during the years he spent growing up in New York City, but none had been like this man. His parents had taken him to church every Sunday without fail, and he had listened to countless sermons by various men of the cloth. Frequently, his mother had invited the ministers over for meals. He remembered them as serious but lighthearted men who enjoyed a fine cigar and a good laugh as much as the next person. None had been as exacting as Reverend John Burke. None had Burke's knack for rubbing folks the wrong way.

Ahead Nate spied their lodge, constructed by Winona and seven of her relatives and friends. The women had sewn together the buffalo-hide cover after he had collected the long, straight saplings needed for the frame and trimmed the trees of all their small branches. One of Winona's kin was a skilled lodge-maker, and under her supervision, with Winona providing plenty of food and the rest supplying plenty of gossip, the 12 hides used had been stitched together in under a day.

This had taken place three years ago. Until that time, whenever Nate and Winona visited the Shoshones, they had stayed with her aunt, Morning Dove, the wife of Spotted Bull. But Nate had tired of imposing on the kindness of her relatives, and had had the lodge built so his family could stay as long as they wanted in the privacy and comfort of their own dwelling. When it was time to leave for their log cabin near Long's Peak, they would dismantle the lodge and drag it home behind their pack animals on several travois.

Nate halted near the entrance and scanned the camp, seeking sign of their black dog, Samson, a mongrel brute capable of holding its own against a panther. As usual the dog was nowhere to be seen. It was the most independent-minded, contrary critter he had ever come across. More than likely it was off in the forest somewhere chasing rabbits or bothering the squirrels, its favorite pastime.

Burke reined up and sniffed. "Are we all staying in this puny wigwam? Won't it be terribly crowded?"

"A wigwam, Reverend, is the kind of lodge the Ottawas, Ojibwas, and other tribes back East live in," Nate corrected him. "These lodges are called teepees."

"Wigwam. Teepee. What difference does it make?" Burke asked, dismounting. "It still promises to be crowded." Bending over, he entered without so much as a by-your-leave.

Nate was about to follow him when Winona clutched his elbow and leaned over to whisper in his ear.

"Later, my husband, you have explaining to do. A *lot* of explaining."

Chapter Seven

As it turned out, his explanation had to wait. They unloaded the bear hide and meat, picketed the horses near their lodge, and were just settling in when a tremendous ruckus broke out on the west side of the village. Nate was the first out of the lodge, his Hawken in his right hand. The sun had dipped below the high mountains to the west, shrouding the Rockies in twilight except for vivid streaks of red and orange framing the horizon.

From harsh experience Nate knew that just before sunrise and right after sunset were the times most favored by roving war parties to conduct their raids. Before the sun came up few warriors were fully awake. After sunset most of the men were in their lodges awaiting their suppers, fatigued after a hard day of work. In particular the Blackfeet, those widely dreaded scourges of the plains and the mountains, liked to strike when their enemies were most vulnerable. So when he heard a Shoshone shouting that each man should arm himself, he figured the Blackfeet must be up to their old, nasty tricks.

Beaver Tail appeared to the north, running toward the source of the noise.

"Do you know what is happening?" Nate asked.

"Bloods," the young warrior replied.

Nate rested his free hand on a flintlock. The Bloods were almost as bad as the Blackfeet. Those two tribes, plus a third known as the Piegans, had formed a confederacy of sorts and were continually waging war against everyone else. He had started to go see for himself when Winona and Zach emerged.

"I heard that," she declared. "You be careful."

"I will," Nate vowed, and looked at his son. "You stay by your mother's side and keep your bow handy in case some of the Bloods sneak into the village while I'm gone."

"Don't worry none, Pa. I'll part their hair if they show their faces."

"And I will keep an eye on our guest," Winona added icily.

"Thanks," Nate said, glad Burke had curled up on a hide the moment he'd entered the lodge and fallen instantly asleep. As exhausted as the minister was, Nate expected him to slumber until morning or later. He sprinted toward a throng of Shoshones near the lake shore.

"Grizzly Killer! Wait for me!"

He looked over his shoulder to find Touch the Clouds close on his heels. The giant held an enormous bow made of ash and had a large brown quiver strapped to his broad back. Side by side they ran to the shore, where a lean warrior was being besieged by questions as everyone tried to talk at once.

"How many were there, Otter Eyes?" asked one man.

"Where did you see them?" wanted to know another.

"Were they on horseback or on foot?"

"Did they try to kill you?"

Touch the Clouds stepped forward. "One at a time! How can he tell us what happened with all of you jabbering like women?" He moved through the excited warriors, towering over every single one of them, his mere presence serving to calm them down. When he reached Otter Eyes, he motioned for complete silence. "Now then. Tell those of us who arrived late what took place."

"There is not much to tell," Otter Eyes said. "I was bringing my horses to water when I saw two men at the edge of those trees and yelled to them, thinking they were friends." He pointed at the forest 20 yards away. "Instead of answering me, they ran off. As they did, I saw by their hair that they were Bloods. So I gave the alarm."

Nate stared at the woods. The deepening darkness made a shadowy maze of the many trunks and thickets. It would be difficult to identify anyone, let alone tell the difference between Shoshones and Bloods. Not that he suspected Otter Eyes was lying. But it might be that the warrior had simply seen a pair of Shoshones going off for some reason and mistaken them for enemies. He saw Touch the Clouds gaze in the same direction, his forehead creased in thought, and figured the giant had reached the same conclusion.

"We should go after them!" Beaver Tail cried. "We must not let them spy on us and get away with it! What if they were part of a large war party? This minute they must be on their way back to tell their friends exactly where to find our village."

Cries of agreement erupted from a dozen throats. Weapons were waved overhead and war whoops cut the air. Several men headed for the forest, but a sharp command brought them all to a halt.

"Stop! Have you taken leave of your senses?" Touch the Clouds demanded. "If there is a war party out there and all of you go rushing off into the woods, who will protect our families and our horses if the war party gets past you?"

The sheepish expressions on some of the Shoshones' faces were so comical Nate had to suppress a grin.

"It will soon be too dark to see anything," Touch the Clouds went on. "I say we have men stand guard until morning, then look for tracks and follow them."

Deliberations ensued as the warriors debated the merits of the idea. Nate placed the stock of his Hawken on the ground and leaned on the barrel, idly listening. He agreed with Touch the Clouds and knew the rest would too, given five or ten minutes of squabbling. Unlike whites, whose armies had clearly defined chains of command and were models of military precision, Indians seldom obeyed any single leader and did as they pleased whether at war or not. It was, in his estimation, their single greatest weakness.

Nate knew how the tribes east of the Mississippi had been treated by his own kind. Those that hadn't been enslaved had been wiped out, and those that hadn't been wiped out had been forced to relocate to less desirable land when envious whites decided they wanted the choice parcels for themselves. Indians had been on the continent before the arrival of the first Europeans, yet the Europeans saw fit to deny the natives citizenship when they formed their governments and divided the land. As a result, the Indians became despised and belittled outcasts, treated more like animals than human beings.

One of Nate's biggest fears was that someday the same thing would happen to the tribes west of the Mississippi. The idea seemed preposterous, but a clash would be inevitable if the population of the United States kept growing at its current rate. Already there were settlers heading for the rich new lands in Oregon country.

He hoped he wouldn't live to see the day when towns and cities sprang up on the prairie and in the mountains. If they did, it would bring to an end the way of life he cherished so dearly and forever put a limit on the freedom he valued as much as life itself.

So far he knew of only two or three trappers who shared his concerns. One was his mentor and best friend, Shakespeare McNair. Shakespeare had lived in the Rockies longer than any white man and, until recently, had been remarkably active for a man of his advanced years. Lately, though, McNair had taken to spending all his time at his cabin in the company of his Flathead wife. Lord, how Nate missed him! He toyed with the notion of paying a visit on his way home, then abruptly realized Touch the Clouds was speaking.

"I will be one of the first to stand guard. Who else will volunteer? There should be at least ten if we are to protect our village properly." He paused. "How about you, Grizzly Killer? Are you with me?"

Nate hesitated. After being gone all day he wanted to spend time with his family. And he didn't like the thought of Winona and Zach being left alone with Reverend Burke. He knew very little about the man, and the little he did know did not inspire trust. The minister, though, should sleep the night through. And Nate's desire to be with his loved ones had to be weighed against the welfare of the entire tribe. There really was no choice. "All right," he responded. "I will gladly do my part."

Immediately other warriors offered to help, and Touch the Clouds picked those he needed. Chief Broken Paw stood close to the giant but made no effort to interfere. Touch the Clouds was the best warrior in the Shoshone village, and in matters of warfare his judgment usually prevailed.

Nate was thinking that he would like to stand guard several hundred yards to the east, to be nearer his lodge, when Touch the Clouds came over and leaned down so only he could hear.

"Thank you, my friend. I was afraid some of the others would object to my idea and we would argue for a long time." He glanced around to be certain no one was trying to eavesdrop. "Crooked Antler had that look in his eyes."

Nate understood. Crooked Antler was the second best warrior in the tribe, and he saw fit to constantly oppose Touch the Clouds. Whether sparked by jealousy or petty revenge because Touch the Clouds had counted more coup and received more honors, the one-sided feud had been going on for two years or better and everyone in the village was aware of it. Crooked Antler was spiteful but he wasn't stupid; he was always careful not to push the giant too far, not to step over that invisible line that would result in a personal challenge. In a fight to the death he wouldn't stand a chance and he knew it.

"I called on you first because your word carries great weight with our people," Touch the Clouds was saying. "Even though you are white, you are considered a fearless warrior whose good medicine is better than anyone else's."

Nate chuckled. "Has some trapper sold you a bottle of whiskey?"

"I am serious, my friend," the giant asserted. "Everyone knows of your battles with the Blackfeet and the Utes. And no man since time began has killed as many of the great brown bears as you have. Your good medicine is extremely powerful." He absently scratched his forehead. "Which is very surprising since you do not even own a medicine bundle."

"I have been lucky," Nate said, and meant it. Most of his narrow escapes and victories over his enemies had been the result of dumb luck. But he could see how the Shoshones regarded him as a man possessing mighty medicine. To them, a man made his own luck by appealing to the invisible spirits for good medicine that would protect him from harm and ill fortune. Many warriors owned what were called medicine bundles, consisting of ordinary objects such as feathers, pipes, tobacco, or something else they might have seen in a dream and believed would give them special powers such as warding off the arrows of their enemies or keeping them in good health forever. There were even tribal medicine bundles. He had heard the Arapahos revered a bundle containing a flat pipe that was kept in a special lodge and watched over by a devoted keeper who made sure the bundle was always hung in the exact center of the lodge and never, ever allowed it to touch the ground.

"I know better," Touch the Clouds said. "You are talking like a white man, not a Shoshone. Your medicine is very powerful, and if you ever make a medicine bundle you will grow very rich by selling some of your power."

That idea had never occurred to Nate. Sometimes, no matter how hard a warrior tried, he was unable to see any visions or have any significant dreams. In such instances the warrior often went to another man noted for having good medicine and bought some of the contents of the man's medicine bundle, or perhaps the entire bundle, so he would have his own good medicine.

Touch the Clouds turned and addressed the others, asking for warriors to volunteer to stand watch during the second half of the night.

Nate felt his stomach growl. He was very hungry, but he wouldn't get a chance to fill his belly until about midnight, when he would be relieved. Resigned to his fate, he waited as those warriors who were not standing guard on the first watch departed for their lodges.

The giant faced him. "If there are Bloods in the area, I doubt they will raid us before dawn. But if they do, our weakest points are here and a ways to the south where the forest is thickest. If you will stand guard here, I will take the other spot."

So much for a place closer to Winona and Zach! Nate wryly reflected. He sighed, then said, "As you wish."

Touch the Clouds had actually bestowed an honor on him by asking him to protect one of the two approaches a war party would be most likely to use. The request was, in effect, a public testimonial to his courage and reliability, as the eight warriors who were staring at him clearly recognized.

In pairs and one by one the others drifted toward their positions around the camp. The giant hiked southward, pausing once to smile and wave, his teeth white in the murky night.

Nate stretched and gazed up at the multitude of stars sparkling in the firmament. A cool breeze from the northwest fanned his cheeks. Water gently lapped at the edge of the lake shore not six feet from his moccasins. The nearest lodge was better than 40 feet to the south. About 20 yards in front of him loomed the inky wall of vegetation that might conceal lurking Bloods. If they should spring a surprise attack, he would be on his own until the Shoshones rallied to defend their village. Like Touch the Clouds, he doubted the Bloods would do anything before dawn. But he had to stay alert anyway. The life of every man, woman, and child was riding on his shoulders.

He moved nearer to the water and along the shore another five yards, then knelt. Now he was close enough to the trees to be able to detect anyone moving across the open space between the lake and the woods and sound the alarm. Or so he hoped. The Bloods were bound to be experts at snaking silently toward an enemy encampment. It was unlikely he would have much forewarning of their presence before he spotted them.

Both flintlocks were wedged under his belt and he had his knife and tomahawk with him. His buckskins and beaver hat would keep him warm, so except for his protesting stomach he would be comfortable while he waited for midnight and his relief. Boredom might be his biggest problem.

Suddenly, as if to prove him wrong, a twig cracked in the forest.

Chapter Eight

Nate froze, probing the forest for movement. He didn't have to look very hard. A shadowy form materialized, advancing from the trees and moving directly toward the lodges. As near as he could tell, there was only one man. Quietly placing the Hawken down, he drew his big butcher knife and slinked forward. If he could capture the Blood alive, the Shoshones might be able to wring important information from him, such as how many were in the raiding party and where they were.

The vague figure made no attempt to conceal himself. Cocky devil, Nate thought, easing onto all fours with the knife clutched tight in his right hand. He angled to one side of the warrior's line of travel, then flattened and tensed for the spring.

On came the Blood, armed with a lance that he was holding at waist height instead of ready to use in combat.

Nate was amazed at the man's careless attitude, but he had no time to dwell on it. In seconds the Blood was

passing him, and he let the warrior take two strides before
he surged upright and pounced, his left arm looping around
the man's neck and clamping down hard so the Blood
couldn't cry out even as he pressed the tip of his blade
into the man's right cheek and growled in Shoshone,
"Make one move and you are dead."

The warrior started to struggle and gurgled as if drown-
ing.

"Do you understand?" Nate demanded, applying more
pressure and digging the knife in deeper. Immediately the
man dropped his lance and ceased resisting. Nate slowly
turned, forcing the Blood to move with him, self-conscious
about having his back to the woods when there undoubtedly were more Bloods somewhere in the vicinity. He
scanned the tree line but saw nothing. Should he shout to
bring the Shoshones on the run? Or was it wiser to keep
quiet so the war party didn't realize one of their own had
been captured?

He headed south, pushing the Blood before him, his left
forearm locked on the man's throat, his knife providing
incentive for the warrior to cooperate. For over a minute
he walked, constantly scouring the forest, barely paying
attention to his prisoner, more concerned over getting an
arrow or lance in the back than over the man giving him
any trouble.

From out of the darkness came a walking mountain.
Touch the Clouds appeared like a wraith out of nowhere,
making no sound whatsoever. "Grizzly Killer?" he whispered. "Is that you?"

"Yes," Nate confirmed. "And I have caught one."

The giant came closer, peered into the prisoner's face,
and made a sound like a bull elk startled by a stalking
panther. "Have you taken a good look at your captive?"

"No. Why?"

"Perhaps you should."

Nate relaxed the pressure on the warrior's throat Just

enough so he could lean forward and see the man's features. Recognition took a second in the dark, but when he saw who it was he lowered his arms and stepped back. "Beaver Tail!"

The young warrior rubbed his throat and glanced from the giant to Nate. "You are strong, Grizzly Killer. I feared you would snap my neck before you learned it was I."

"You're fortunate I didn't shoot you on sight or slit you from ear to ear," Nate said. "What were you doing out in the forest?"

"The forest?" Touch the Clouds repeated.

Beaver Tail fidgeted nervously. "Yes. I wanted to see if there were Bloods nearby, so when you were talking and everyone was busy listening I sneaked off into the trees."

"You young fool," Touch the Clouds said sternly. "What if there had been a war party out there? What chance would you have had all alone? You took a needless risk."

"Which is easy for you to say," Beaver Tail replied. "You have counted more coup than ten men. You have no need to prove yourself. But what about those of us who have yet to count our first coup?"

Nate slid his knife into its sheath. The young man's motive was perfectly logical given the intense competition among the warriors to see who could garner the most honors in battle. To count coup a warrior would do practically anything: rush headlong into enemy fire, fight against overwhelming odds, even stake himself to the ground so that he couldn't leave the battlefield before all his enemies had turned tail or were dead.

"Patience, my friend," Touch the Clouds advised, draping a hand on Beaver Tail's shoulder. "You must have patience. Your time to count coup will come soon enough. Losing your hair in the meantime because you are too rash for your own good will make your name a laughingstock instead of one our women will speak with pride.'' He patted Beaver Tail's arm. ''When you have been in as many terrible fights as I have, when you have seen so many honorable men die horrible deaths, many of them your best friends, you will not be so thirsty for blood.''

''I will not rest until I have counted more coup than any Shoshone who ever lived!'' Beaver Tail declared. Pivoting, he hastened toward the lodges, his back stiff, his chin thrust defiantly outward.

Touch the Clouds watched him go. ''I have often wondered why the Great Medicine saw fit to make men so ignorant and childish. By the time we are old enough to figure out the way of the world, we are ready for the grave.''

Nate had no answer for that one. ''I should get back to my post,'' he said, thinking of his rifle, and began to retrace his steps. Hindsight told him it had been a mistake to go off and leave his Hawken behind. Not that any of the Shoshones would steal it. Few of them liked to use guns. Most preferred using their traditional bows and arrows over the white man's weapon, with good reason since a skilled archer could fire anywhere from ten to 20 shafts in the time it took the average trapper to reload. Then too, he had carved his initials on the stock and would have no problem identifying his own rifle.

Just being separated from the Hawken made him feel uncomfortable. A man's rifle was as essential to his continued existence as breathing itself, more so than a brace of pistols. Flintlocks were fine for close-in fighting and for shooting small game at close range. But for dropping bigger animals like buffalo, elk, and deer, at great distances, and for keeping hostiles at bay, there was nothing like a dependable Hawken.

He made for the approximate spot where he had jumped Beaver Tail, then walked to where he had deposited the rifle. It wasn't there. Bending over so he could see the ground better, he searched to the right and the left. He wasn't worried. He had simply misjudged the proper spot by a few feet or so and would find the rifle any moment.

A minute elapsed and he saw no trace of it. Puzzled, he straightened near the water and put his hands on his hips as he tried to deduce where he was going wrong. How could he be so far off the mark? Had he been farther east or west when he set the weapon down? In the excitement of seeing a presumed enemy, he might not have been as observant as he should have been.

Chiding himself for being such a dunderhead, he angled to the west, stooped low to examine every square inch of grass and dirt. If he failed to find the weapon in another minute or two, he would go to the nearest lodge and ask the warrior inside for a burning brand from the cooking fire. Weaving back and forth, he went closer to the trees. When he turned toward the village, he finally found his Hawken. But not in the way he expected.

The patter of rushing feet made Nate uncoil and spin, his right hand swooping to his flintlock. He saw a stocky shape an instant before something slammed into his forehead with the force of a runaway ten-ton boulder. Bright pinpoints of light blossomed before his eyes. And then the darkness claimed more than the land. It claimed his mind.

The tantalizing odor of roasting deer meat was the first sensation Nate became conscious of. He lay still, taking stock, aware he was on his back on the ground and a rock was gouging him in the lower back. His arms rested on his chest, his wrists were bound. Gruff voices spoke in a tongue he didn't know, but which he suspected was the language of the Bloods. His head throbbed. It hurt just to think. Otherwise, he seemed to be fine.

Cracking his eyelids, he peered at a group of seven Blood warriors gathered around a crackling fire over which a haunch of venison was roasting. Trees ringed them, leading him to surmise they were in a clearing in the forest. Through the trunks he spied the sun rising above the far horizon. Apparently he had been out all night long and now a new day was dawning. He could hear birds chirping and the chattering of an irate squirrel.

One of the Bloods, an imposing figure who wore three eagle feathers in his long hair, rose and came toward him.

Nate closed his eyes and feigned being unconscious. He involuntarily flinched when a sharp object jabbed him in the side. The warrior spoke a few words, then jabbed him again, only harder. There was nothing to be gained by pretending any longer, so Nate opened his eyes and stared up into the Blood's impassive face.

In the warrior's right hand was a hunting knife. He slid it into a sheath on his right hip before addressing Nate again. A second warrior, shorter and with a cleft chin, came over.

Nate didn't understand a word. "Do you speak Shoshone?" he asked when the warrior fell silent.

Neither Blood responded.

"How about English?" Nate inquired in that language.

Again the Bloods showed no indication they comprehended. They conversed briefly in their own tongue, then the one wearing the eagle feathers lifted his hands. "If you speak sign, white man, nod once."

Nate nodded. The shorter Blood drew a knife and leaned down to slice the rope binding his wrists.

"If you try to escape we will kill you here and now," the taller warrior signed. "I am Eagle Claw of the Bloods. Who are you, white man? And what were you doing at the Shoshone camp?"

Slowly sitting up, Nate rubbed his wrists to restore the circulation, then noticed the rest of the war party approaching. Two held bows, arrows nocked and ready to fly. He must make no unwarranted moves or he would never see his wife and son again. "I am known as Grizzly Killer," he signed. "The Shoshones are my adopted people."

Eagle Claw and the one with the cleft chin talked in their tongue for a bit. Finally, Eagle Claw looked down at him and said, "Are you the same Grizzly Killer who slew Mad Dog and White Bear of the Blackfeet?"

Nate answered honestly. Lying would do no good since he was the only white man in the entire Rocky Mountains who was called by that name. Occasionally Indian men from different tribes had the same name, but there were so few whites in the mountains that every name applied to only one person. "I am," he said.

Eagle Claw frowned. "The Blackfeet are our brothers."

"I know."

"Their enemies are our enemies."

"So I have heard," Nate said. The confederacy between the Blackfeet, Bloods, and Piegans was loose-knit in that they rarely conducted raids together or combined their forces to wage war, but whoever aroused the anger of one tribe incurred the wrath of all three.

"Then you must also know that we will slay you."

"You will try."

Eagle Claw's eyes narrowed, then he clapped his hands and burst into hearty laughter. Some of the others joined in, but not the warrior with the cleft chin. He glowered, insulted by Nate's audacity.

"You have courage, white man," Eagle Claw signed when the rough mirth subsided. "I will grant you that. But even brave men die."

"The measure of a man is how well he dies," Nate signed, choosing his words carefully, seeking to impress the Bloods and buy himself a fighting chance. "Cowards whine and cry. Brave men like us go to the spirit world with our heads held high." He paused, gazing at each of them in turn. "All I ask is a fair chance, and I believe you will give it to me because the Bloods are widely regarded as some of the fiercest fighters of all the tribes in this land. Surely you would not stake me out to die in the hot sun like the Comanches might do, or tie me and fill me with arrows like the Apaches. Such deaths give no honor to anyone. Let me run a gauntlet. Or have me fight as many of you as you wish using only knives or tomahawks. Just let me die with dignity.''

At a gesture from Eagle Claw, the Bloods stepped closer to the fire and began a lively discussion.

Had the plea worked? Nate wondered hopefully. Indian men regarded bravery as the highest of virtues, and they regarded dying in battle as the ideal way to give up the ghost. No warrior wanted to die a helpless victim. He tried to read their feelings by their expressions but it was impossible. Eagle Claw and the one with the cleft chin were arguing strenuously while the others listened.

He suddenly spotted his weapons lying in a pile to the right of the fire. The flintlocks were on top. If he took a half-dozen quick strides, he could snatch them up and cut loose. But he knew those two Bloods with bows would both put arrows into him before he got off a single shot. He would live longer if he did nothing for the time being.

Eagle Claw was coming toward him. "Your eloquent words have touched our hearts, white man. All of us except Kicking Bird agree a man should have a fighting chance when he dies. Kicking Bird says that you are white and don't deserve to leave this world like a true man. He says you should die like a dog.''

Nate glanced at the warrior with the cleft chin, who gave him a look of pure murderous venom.

"So you will get your wish," Eagle Claw signed.

"How is it to be?" Nate asked.

The leader of the war party grinned enigmatically. "We want that to be a surprise.''

Chapter Nine

Nate didn't like the fact that most of the Bloods then laughed and one made motions suggestive of a body being ripped to shreds, which prompted more laughter. Even Kicking Bird smiled, which confirmed the manner of death they had chosen must be particularly fiendish.

"We are about to have our breakfast," Eagle Claw signed. "Would you care for some deer meat?"

Surprised by the unexpected generosity, Nate licked his lips and signed, "Yes, please."

"A wise decision. You will soon need all of your strength," Eagle Claw said, and went to the fire.

One of the Bloods carved large pieces off the roast and passed them out to the others. He also brought a fist-sized chunk to Nate. The warriors sat down to eat, the pair with bows taking their seats with their backs to the flames so they could keep their eyes on their captive.

Rather than uselessly dwell on his impending fate, Nate ate with relish. He was famished, the deer meat delicious.

His piece included a wide strip of fat which he chewed on greedily, savoring the tangy taste. In his estimation animal fat was even better than the meat itself. When he was done he licked his fingers clean and smacked his lips, Indian fashion, to show the meal had been a good one.

The Bloods appeared surprised by his casual attitude. They soon had something else to occupy their attention, however; they divided up his weapons among them. Eagle Claw took the Hawken, and the rest of the band drew lots to see who would get what. Kicking Bird ended up with one of the flintlocks. To antagonize Nate, he held the gun out where Nate could see it and repeatedly stroked the barrel while smirking smugly.

Nate wished he could find a way of taking that bastard with him when he went. The sun was well above the horizon, and his intuition told him it wouldn't be much longer before the Bloods sprang their little surprise.

Minutes later Eagle Claw stood. The fire was hurriedly extinguished, each man gathered up his weapons, and in single file they hiked to the northwest. Nate was forced to walk between Kicking Bird and one of the bowmen. Like the Blackfeet, the Bloods rarely rode horses when on raids. They preferred to travel afoot and strike swiftly and silently.

It was a beautiful morning. Sunlight streamed through the branches overhead, bathing the grass and wild flowers in golden radiance. Sparrows flitted about in the undergrowth. Jays flew from tree to tree seeking food. And, as always, chipmunks were everywhere, darting to and fro.

Nate's headache evaporated after they had gone a mile. The invigorating mountain air and the exercise cleared his head and primed his senses for the ordeal to come. He kept looking for a chance to bolt for freedom, but the Blood behind him was as vigilant as a hawk.

Almost an hour after leaving the clearing they entered a verdant valley and marched up it to an ominous bald mountain. Huge shadows from drifting clouds shaded the higher elevations. The lower portion consisted of sheer cliffs and jumbled boulder fields where nothing grew. Desolate and bleak, the mountain was a barren contrast to the sea of life swirling all around it.

Eagle Claw walked back to Nate. "Do you know this mountain, white man?"

"No," Nate signed.

"My people call it the Mountain Where Evil Spirits Dwell. A long time ago one of our warriors was catching eagles up near the top when a strange wind came up and blew him over a cliff. When his friends found his body, they discovered it had been split in half. Since then we never go up there."

Craning his neck, Nate gazed at the rocky heights and spied a lone eagle soaring regally on the currents. He had once helped a Ute gather eagle feathers, and knew firsthand how difficult the task was. The favored technique consisted in digging a hole for a man to hide in, then constructing a latticework cover of thin limbs camouflaged with clods of grass and dirt. A warrior would stake out the bait, usually a dead rabbit, next to the hole and climb in. When an eagle dived down for the kill, the man would quickly reach out and grab the big bird's legs with one hand, then rapidly pluck feathers with the other. The warrior had to work swiftly since it was impossible to hold the enraged bird for long. Occasionally a man would lose a finger or an eye, and all for a handful of the most prized feathers an Indian could own. It would be much easier to simply shoot an eagle, but to the Indian way of thinking that would be a terrible waste of life. "Let me guess," he signed. "You want me to climb up there so the wind will blow me off?"

"No," Eagle Claw said, grinning. "We have another end in mind for you." Again he took the lead and they wound into a narrow ravine.

Nate paused once to scan the steep stone sides, and felt the tip of an arrow poke him in the spine. He walked on, perplexed, unable to deduce their intent. The ground was too rocky to bear tracks, so he had no idea whether the Bloods had ever been up the ravine before or not. He got the impression, though, they knew exactly where they were going.

The ravine twisted and turned like a sidewinder, eventually broadening out at the base of a high cliff on the south side of the foreboding mountain. Boulders the size of log cabins flanked the cliff, obscuring the lower section from view.

Nate reluctantly let himself be led into the boulder field. A glint of white to his left made him glance around, and there in the dust lay the leg bone of an elk, the bone bearing numerous teeth marks. He hadn't gone ten feet when he spotted another one, this time the thigh bone. Farther on he saw the complete skeleton of a young mountain sheep, the skull lying several feet from the rib section. Most of the rib bones had been cracked off and gnawed on.

Budding apprehension flowed through Nate. Where there were this many bones, there must be the lair of a predator nearby. In this instance it was most likely a panther—or mountain lion as some called the big cats. Was that their destination? He hardly thought so. The panther was just as apt to attack them as him.

He saw Eagle Claw slow, then stop in the shelter of a huge boulder. A warrior armed with a lance moved stealthily forward and disappeared. The others waited in silence. "What is going on?" he inquired.

"You will see soon enough, white dog," Kicking Bird answered. "And when you do, perhaps you will change your mind about wanting a fighting chance. If so, if you admit you are a coward and not a true man, I will make your end swift and painless." He tapped the hilt of his knife, then drew a finger across his throat.

Nate resented being taunted. "There is only one coward here and he goes by the name of Kicking Bird." He detected a blur of motion a fraction of a second before his own flintlock struck him flush on the jaw. Lanced with pain, suddenly dizzy, he tottered and sank to his knees. Dimly, he heard harsh words spoken in whispers. When his vision cleared he saw Eagle Claw and another warrior restraining a furious Kicking Bird, who had cocked the pistol and was trying to point the barrel in his direction.

Kicking Bird gradually regained his self-control. He let the hammer down and barked a few words. His arms were released and he shoved the flintlock under the top of his leggings. His countenance mirrored volcanic hatred of Nate.

Wondering why they were all whispering, Nate slowly stood. Were they so near the predator's lair that they risked being heard and attacked? And what manner of predator would make a band of otherwise fearless Bloods behave like timid children?

In strained silence the warriors waited for their companion with the lance to return. Five minutes later he did, speaking urgently but softly to Eagle Claw, who pursed his lips and gave Nate a long, searching look.

What were they up to? Nate asked himself yet again. Kicking Bird was grinning at him, as if at a private joke. Whatever they had in mind must be typically devious and especially gruesome. Indians shared few of the qualms white men possessed about inflicting truly barbarous deaths on their enemies. Indeed, Indians victorious in battle often inflicted the most appalling atrocities on their captives to see how well the unfortunates held up. It wasn't that Indians delighted in torture. Torture was simply a test of bravery. Those taken prisoner knew what to expect and would do the same if the situation was reversed.

Eagle Claw took the lead again, Nate's Hawken held firmly in his hands.

The band wound deeper into the field of mammoth boulders, winding ever nearer the base of the bald mountain. Nate saw more bones. Lots more. In vain he hunted for tracks, for any clue as to the identity of the creature responsible, but the rocky ground was a blank page.

After three minutes of travel the Bloods slowed. This time two warriors were sent ahead while the band waited.

"It will not be long now, Grizzly Killer," Kicking Bird signed with a sneer.

"Until what?" Nate responded.

"Be patient, white dog," Kicking Bird said, and added mockingly, "Are you still feeling brave? Or are you ready to admit that all your talk of dying bravely was the talk of a weakling stalling for time in the hope you could escape?"

"You will see how brave I am when the time comes," Nate signed, then grinned. Here he was, sparring words with the Blood just as a shoshone would. In some ways he was more Indian than he realized,

"You find this humorous?" Kicking Bird asked.

"I find you humorous," Nate answered. "Until I met you, I had no idea that Blood men like to work their mouths more than their brains. I am quite amazed the Blackfeet would accept your tribe as allies."

Kicking Bird bristled, his hand swooping to the flintlock. For a moment he was on the verge of drawing. But he checked himself with a visible effort and relaxed his grip. "The only reason I do not kill you here and now is because I know what is in store for you and I do not want to deprive myself of the satisfaction of hearing you scream and plead for your miserable life."

Eagle Claw walked up to them and signed to Nate. "Why do you persist in insulting him? Kicking Bird is noted for his fiery temper. If you are not careful, he will shoot you where you stand."

"This white dog wants me to," Kicking Bird signed

using sharp, angry gestures. "He hopes I will spare him from his deserved fate, but he will be disappointed. I want to watch him die in intense agony. I want to see his guts ripped from his body and hear the crunch of his bones as—"

"Enough!" Eagle Claw interrupted. "You will spoil our surprise."

"My apology," Kicking Bird said.

Nate couldn't resist the opening. "There is no need to apologize. We all understand how children like to make idle boasts."

A flinty gleam came into Kicking Bird's eyes. "I have never looked forward to the death of an enemy with so much anticipation as I look forward to yours."

At that juncture the two warriors returned on the run. The Bloods clustered together and exchanged whispered words for several minutes. Eventually the pair with bows took up positions behind Nate and Eagle Claw motioned for him to start walking.

High above them reared the stark, jagged mountain, shrouded in shadows from passing clouds. Nate guessed they were within 50 yards of a towering cliff scarred by deep cracks and broken sections, toward which they were evidently heading. The Bloods were exercising great care, halting behind each boulder to survey the route ahead and crossing open spaces swiftly. He could practically feel their anxious tension.

He glanced back at the grim bowmen, who had him covered with their shafts, and frowned. It had been a mistake not to attempt to escape sooner. Now he must either commit virtual suicide by making a bid for his freedom or accept the inevitable and face whatever lay ahead. There was always the slim chance he might be able to slay the creature and then effect his escape. The sight of more bones, this time those of a bear, gave him second thoughts. The size of the bear's partially crushed skull revealed it had been between two and four years of age, not a cub by any means, in the prime of its vigor and strength.

Nate licked his lips and rubbed his moist palms together. What was capable of slaying a grown bear? He began to wonder if the creature might be of an unknown species, one he had never encountered. All tribes had legends of monsters, many dating from the times of antiquity when the Indians first settled on the North American continent. Most involved tales of heroic warriors who fought and vanquished ferocious beasts unlike any currently alive. And too, he recalled his own harrowing experience not long ago in a hidden valley far to the north where he had nearly lost his life to The Thing That Lurks in the Dark, as the Crows called the mysterious denizen of that valley.

Suddenly his reflection was brought to an end; they emerged from the boulder field less than 30 yards from the base of the cliff. Between them and the rock face the ground sloped down to form a huge bowl. They stood on the rim, surveying the erosion-formed depression. In front of them and to the left the earth walls of the bowl were ten to 15 feet high. To the right was an earthen ramp extending from the top to the bottom. The opposite side was actually the cliff itself, and at its base was the entrance to a cave, a murky opening a dozen feet high and equally as wide.

Nate took all this in at a glance. His main attention was riveted on the scores of skeletons littering the bowl floor. He recognized bones from all sorts of animals. Whatever killed them must have an insatiable appetite. The cave, he realized with a start, had to be the creature's lair. He had started to take a step backwards away from the edge when a rough pair of hands rammed into his shoulder blades and he was brutally shoved over the brink.

Chapter Ten

Nate instinctively threw out his arms to balance himself as he fell. He felt fleeting surprise, and then the ground was rushing up to meet him and he had to concentrate on relaxing as he hit to better absorb the shock and save his legs from injury. Too late he saw the bones of an elk directly under him. He tried to slant to one side but his momentum was too great. The soles of his feet slammed down onto the elk's rib cage and he heard a loud crack as one of the ribs snapped off. Jarring pain shot up his left leg. In a twinkling he was pitched to the left, onto his side, and he landed hard on his left arm, jarring the elbow and causing his arm to go numb.

For a few seconds he lay there, gathering his wits. His blood raced in his veins, his heart pounded in his chest. Now he knew why Kicking Bird had looked forward to his death with such relish. The Bloods were counting on whatever lived in the cave to do the same to him as it had done to countless wild animals. They were giving him his fighting chance, all right, against a monster that killed for food.

Nate pushed to his knees and glanced at the cave mouth, expecting to see a hideous nightmare appear. But nothing moved in the lair. Perhaps it was nocturnal and slept during the day. If he moved quickly he could run up the ramp and get the hell out of there before the thing came out.

He pushed upright and winced as pain lanced his left ankle. Was it broken? Taking a few tentative steps, he concluded he had suffered a mild sprain, which was the least of his worries given the circumstances. He turned toward the ramp and broke into a shuffling run, covering five yards before he heard a buzzing sound and an arrow thudded into the dirt at his feet.

Nate looked up. The seven Bloods, all smiles, were still perched on the rim. Both warriors with bows were set to loose a shaft again should he attempt to use the ramp. They had him right where they wanted him, and now they were going to stand up there and watch as whatever lurked in the cave made a meal of him.

Kicking Bird's hands moved in sign language. "Do you still pretend to have courage, white dog?"

Twisting, Nate glanced at the ramp 20 feet off. So close, yet so far. And there was no other way out. He faced the Bloods again, clenching his fists in fury.

Eagle Claw was holding the Hawken in the crook of his left elbow. "We decided this would be a fitting end for you, Grizzly Killer. Do not worry. If you die well, we will tell our people and spread the word among the Blackfeet and the Piegans. Sooner or later the story will get back to the Shoshones and they will honor your passing." He gazed at the cave. "We have known of Silver Hair for many years. Those who came to this mountain for eagle feathers always gave him and his lair a wide berth."

Silver Hair? They had a name for the monster? Nate

pivoted so he could keep an eye on the cave.

"Silver Hair is the oldest of his kind," Eagle Claw continued in sign. "Some say he has lived forever. Some claim he can never be killed. It is most appropriate that he be the one who kills you."

Why was it so damned fitting? Nate mused, and cast about for a weapon. There were plenty of bones, some heavy thigh bones that would suffice as a club. He saw one that appeared to be sturdy and went over to pick it up.

Deep within the cave, something growled.

A ripple of fear coursed down Nate's back and he froze in the act of reaching for the thigh bone to stare at the cave in dread. Whatever dwelled in there was awake and might be coming out! He grabbed the bone and stepped back, his skin crawling. Low chortles from on high drew him up short. The Bloods were laughing at him! A surge of indignation replaced his fear. Mad at himself for letting abject fright get the better of him, he glared up at the band.

Kicking Bird's shoulders shook with glee.

Nate took a few steps to the left, seeking a spot to make his stand. The scattered bones offered nowhere to conceal himself, so he had no choice but to fight for his life. From out of the cave issued another, louder, growl. The creature was indeed emerging. He hefted the thigh bone, so heavy and yet so puny.

A third growl let him know the monster was close to the entrance.

Nate had rarely felt so helpless. He thought of Winona and Zach and felt profoundly sorry he had failed them. Since a woman was rarely able to live by herself in Indian society, Winona would be forced to find a new husband, even though she had many times asserted that should he die, she would never marry again. And young Zach would be deprived of a father's guidance when he needed it the most.

Something moved in the cave.

Crouching, Nate clutched the end of the thigh bone with both hands and waited, his eyes probing the gloomy confines of the passageway through which the monster was approaching. He could see an enormous bulk moving ponderously outward. It paused just shy of the sunlight and he heard it sniff several times. Then, with measured strides, it advanced into the open.

Nate wished the earth would open up and swallow him. In all his years in the Rockies, in all his run-ins with wild beasts, he had never beheld anything as huge as the stupendous grizzly that now stood and met his gawking gaze with a baleful stare of its own. A colossal creature, it was almost the size of a full-grown buffalo bull. Likewise remarkable was the color of its coat; while grizzlies could be any color from yellowish-brown to almost black, often with white-tipped hairs that gave them their grizzled aspect, this one was solid silver from the tip of its twitching black nose to the end of its stubby tail.

Now Nate understood why the Bloods kept insisting his end would be so appropriate. After all, what could be more fitting for someone named Grizzly Killer than to meet his end under the slashing claws of the biggest grizzly in existence? He glanced up at the rim, thinking the band would be enjoying more laughter at his expense, and was mildly surprised to see they had all flattened and were peeking over the edge to witness the outcome of his battle.

The grizzly had yet to make a threatening move. It was studying him, perhaps confused at finding a human so close to its lair. Nate knew it wouldn't stand still for long. The number of skeletons dotting the bowl and lying among the boulders disclosed this one was an inveterate meat eater, unlike a normal bear. All grizzlies ate meat from time to time, but most would rather dine on berries, fruit, insects, leaves, and twigs. Meat was not their staple. Even when they slew trappers or Indians, they seldom consumed the bodies.

This grizzly was a different story entirely. Sometimes the great bears developed a craving for raw flesh and would eat little else. They would even kill their own kind if another bear strayed onto their territory. The gigantic creature before him was just such a carnivorous monster.

Nate held himself as rigid as a pole. He scarcely breathed. He saw the grizzly sweep its head from side to side, then tilt its head upward to better catch the air currents. There could be no doubt the thing had seen him. So what was it waiting for?

The bear took five steps to its left, halted, and resumed sniffing.

Mystified, Nate waited for the beast to charge. His club might as well be a blade of grass for all the good it would do him. A bear that size would be impervious to any and all blows, except possibly on the face. Once it came at him, he would go for its eyes. Perhaps, if he could temporarily blind it, he might be able to reach the ramp provided the Bloods didn't kill him first. A quick look at the rim confirmed they were still there, seven heads all in a row, most smirking at his expense. What he wouldn't give to be able to turn the tables and have them in his place!

A crazy idea blossomed, a way of possibly diverting the bear's attention from himself to the Bloods. It all depended on the grizzly. Would the beast charge at his slightest move, or would it hold off for ten or 20 seconds, giving him time to put his harebrained scheme into effect?

So far the monster did not appear eager to devour him. Still sniffing, Silver Hair moved to the right.

Nate suddenly had an insight. If the bear had lived in that cave for many years, as the Bloods claimed, then it must be getting on in years, an old-timer well past its prime despite its tremendous size. If so, its eyesight must be extremely poor. Throughout their lives, grizzlies relied extensively on their sense of smell because their vision was inferior even to man's. Advancing years only compounded the problem.

There was a saying among the Shoshones that adequately described the bear's senses. "When a pine cone falls in the forest, the eagle sees it, the deer hears it, and the great brown bear smells it." So now he knew why the colossus was trying so hard to catch his scent. The brute couldn't see him clearly and wasn't quite certain what he was.

Could he use that to his advantage? Nate wondered. He searched the ground around him and saw a shattered skeleton of a deer a couple of yards away. Among the broken bones was a piece the size of his fist. It would be perfect.

Taking a deep breath, Nate darted to the piece and scooped it up. Spinning, his eyes on Silver Hair, he raced toward the wall directly below the Bloods. The grizzly had cocked its head and was regarding him intently. Sheer dread lent speed to Nate's feet. He intentionally avoided looking at the Bloods until the very last instant so they wouldn't guess his intent and scoot from sight to thwart him.

He saw Silver Hair take a step toward him, and then he was right where he wanted to be, 12 feet from the wall, which was as close as he could get due to the angle involved. Abruptly facing the Bloods, he whipped back his right hand and hurled the piece of bone with all the might in his powerful shoulders. Straight at Kicking Bird.

Years of practice tossing rocks and skimming flat stones on the surface of various ponds, rivers, and lakes now paid off. The bone projectile flew true to his aim, striking Kicking Bird full in the face. The startled warrior vented a yelp of pain, and without thinking pushed to his knees, his hands pressed to his bloody nose.

Nate dived, hitting the ground on his elbows and knees, and held himself still. He glanced at the grizzly and nearly laughed in delight. His strategy had worked!

Silver Hair had heard the yelp and was now gazing suspiciously at the rim where Kicking Bird's torso was silhouetted against the backdrop of daylight. The bear advanced a third of the way across the bowl, its nose working like a bellows at a blacksmith's shop.

Nate twisted his head and saw Kicking Bird frozen in place. The warrior was afraid to move for fear the movement would be all that was needed to bring the grizzly up the ramp after him. Nate heard the bear growl, and turned his attention to it just as the monster caught an airborne scent and voiced a roar that shook the walls.

Silver Hair was up and out of the depression in the time it took Nate to blink twice. He never would have suspected the great bear could move so fast. The Bloods were also taken by surprise, and they barely had time to leap to their feet and race for the boulder field before Silver Hair reached the spot where they had been lying. Roaring lustily, the grizzly pursued them.

Nate pushed upright and ran to the ramp. He owed his life to the freakish nature of air currents. In the bottom of the bowl, which the breeze could not reach, there had been no current to carry his scent to the bear. But the breeze *off* the rim had been another story, bringing the scent of the Bloods to Silver Hair's nostrils and arousing the temperamental beast to a state of primal fury at having its sanctuary invaded by hated humankind.

He reached the top of the ramp before he realized he still clasped the thigh bone and cast it aside. The Bloods were almost to the huge boulders, the grizzly hard on their heels. To his consternation, Silver Hair inexplicably stopped and watched the band disappear from view.

The next moment the bear wheeled and started back toward the bowl.

Nate was caught flat-footed. There was no cover between the ramp and the boulders. At any second Silver

Hair would spot him, and in its agitated state, the grizzly would charge whether it detected his scent or not. He turned to the cliff and saw numerous cracks and spots where the rock face had crumpled. Climbing the rock wall was his only hope.

Stepping closer, Nate reached up and inserted his fingers into a crack, then jabbed the toes of his left foot into a groove at waist height. He gripped a second crack with his other hand and pulled himself off the ground just as Silver Hair roared once more.

A look back showed the bear had seen him and was barreling forward, its lips curled back over teeth that could crush a man's bones as easily as a man's teeth could sheer through a slice of bread.

Nate frantically sought another crack, found a suitable one, and clawed upward. If he could get high enough, the grizzly wouldn't be able to get him. Wedging his fingers into a narrow cleft, he rose another few inches. He dared not glance over his shoulder again. The delay might cost him his life.

Five feet he climbed. Then seven. His fingers hurt, his toes too, but he couldn't slow down. A horizontal crack enabled him to gain another foot, but he was still far from safe. He expected to hear the monster closing on him, but heard nothing. Then, as he grabbed for a hole formed when some of the stone had eroded away, he heard a rumbling growl from directly below, and peering between his legs, Nate saw Silver Hair at the base of the cliff. That very instant, the bear lunged upward, its huge forepaw reaching up to rip him from his perch.

Chapter Eleven

For a heartbeat Nate clung to the wall as terror flooded through him. Self-preservation, that most basic of human instincts, came to his rescue just as the grizzly's claws nipped at his left heel. He glanced up, saw an inviting crack a foot above his head, and thrust with both hands, sticking his fingers in as far as they would go. His feet lost their purchase. His body swayed outward, and for several harrowing seconds he thought he would lose his grip and fall on top of the bear.

Silver Hair had put a paw on the cliff face. Snarling, it swiped at Nate's dangling legs but failed to connect.

Mustering all his energy, Nate yanked his feet up and tucked his knees against his stomach. The tormenting strain on his arms and shoulders caused him to grit his teeth. He looked right and left, found a mere bump of rock, and got one foot braced on top of it.

Growling in anger, Silver Hair swung and missed. Not once, but three times, and after the third futile swing the grizzly lowered itself to the earth and began pacing from side to side while staring hungrily upward.

Nate gulped and sought another handhold overhead. Should it occur to the bear to stand on its hind legs and straighten to its full height, he would soon be in the beast's belly. He spied a protruding ridge no more than an inch wide about ten inches above and to the right, and gauged whether he could grip it with a quick flick of his hand. As he girded himself for the attempt, he was stunned to hear sharp retorts of gunfire come from the boulder field, mingled with savage war whoops and frenzied yells.

The grizzly also heard and turned.

Maybe the bear would leave to investigate, Nate hoped. From the sound of things, the Bloods were embroiled in a running battle. But with whom? A likely answer occurred to him and he felt a surge of excitement. It might be his Shoshone friends! The Shoshones could have tracked the Bloods to the vicinity of the bald mountain, then conducted a search when the trail vanished into the ravine.

His joy transformed into horror when Silver Hair began walking toward the boulders. If his friends got past the Bloods, they would have to contend with the monster. "Where are you going?" he bellowed, and whistled shrilly in an effort to keep the bear's attention fixed on him.

The grizzly halted, then swung around.

"That's it, you ugly good-for-nothing!" Nate shouted. "Come after me!"

Silver Hair lumbered back to the bottom of the cliff.

"Don't go anywhere," Nate kept talking. "I want you to stay right there, you flea-ridden sorry excuse for an animal."

Growling hideously, Silver Hair placed both forepaws on the cliff.

"You're too fat to climb!" Nate taunted, and waved his right hand in the air. "You're nothing but a big, hairy pig!" The shooting and the whoops had died down and his friends might appear at any moment. He wanted them to spot the bear before it spotted them.

Silver Hair inched higher, saliva dripping from its jaw.

"If I had my knife I'd show you a thing or two," Nate boasted, continuing to wave his arm to further keep the grizzly distracted. He stared at the boulders, then stiffened as the edge of the crack under his left hand crumbled and his fingers slipped out. In desperation he clutched at the cliff face, but the damage was done. Downward he plummeted.

Nate envisioned falling into the grizzly's gaping maw. Instead, he slammed onto the bear's head, his elbow smashing into hard bone, and then he was falling again, rolling down the bear's back until he struck the ground. He kept rolling, knowing to lie still would result in certain death, trying to make himself a difficult target for the bear to hit. A single swipe of those wicked claws would open him up like an overripe melon.

He rolled and rolled. Oddly, he seemed to be going downhill. The awful truth hit him at the same instant he hit the skeleton of an elk, coming to a gut-wrenching stop, and he shoved to his feet in dismay to find himself once again at the bottom of the bowl. He had rolled back down the ramp!

Silver Hair materialized at the top, the picture of bestial rage.

Nate stumbled rearward. He looked for something he could use as a weapon. To his right was the skull of a white-tailed buck with one antler still attached. Beside it lay the other antler, broken into sections.

Roaring its challenge, the massive grizzly swooped down the incline toward him.

What happened next transpired in a blur of action. Nate didn't think as he moved; he reacted instinctively, automatically, grasping the deer skull and raising it into the air, then waiting, poised to throw, until the bear was almost upon him. He hurled the skull with all of his sinewy might, catching Silver Hair on the brow and bringing the beast to an abrupt halt, really a pause of two or three seconds, just long enough for him to grab part of the broken antler, a straight section six inches long that ended in a tapered point, and to spring in close, wielding the antler like a knife.

The bear saw him leap and opened its mouth wide to bite.

In the fraction of time before Silver Hair could chomp down, Nate speared the tip of the antler into the grizzly's left eye and jerked his arm back. The monster erupted in a volcanic tantrum, roaring and swinging its front paws as it reared onto its hind legs. He glimpsed a paw sweeping at his temple, and then a battering ram collided with his head and he was swatted like a helpless fly, sailing ten feet or more to crash onto his back among the scattered bones.

Dazed, Nate rose on an elbow to see the grizzly swiping at the antler imbedded in its eye. He spotted the leg bone of an elk, one end jagged where the bear had bitten it off to get at the juicy marrow, and scrambled to his feet. In two bounds he had the leg bone in his hands. Whirling, impelled by necessity, he committed an act any normal man would regard as insane. He either fought or he died; so he fought. He charged Silver Hair.

Blood flowed from the grizzly's ruptured eye. It growled and swung, missing by inches, its reflexes dulled by agony and age.

Nate had ducked under that blow. Like a man possessed, he lanced the bone into the grizzly's side but barely dented its thick hide. Sliding to the left, he drove his crude spear up into the underside of the bear's chin where the hide was softer, and this time split it open. He drew back the leg bone to try again, but a huge paw walloped him on the chest and he was knocked off his feet, dimly aware his buckskin shirt had been torn, his flesh cut, the clammy feel of blood on his skin.

He rose slowly this time. Silver Hair was on all fours, moving toward the cave entrance. Suddenly the bear staggered, then sagged onto its forepaws. A thick flow of crimson poured from the stabbed eye.

Nate saw the deer skull and picked it up. His chest smarting abominably, he dashed to the grizzly's side and slammed the skull down on top of Silver Hair's head, flailing away like a madman, striking again and again, pounding until his arms were so tired he couldn't lift the skull. Wearily, he tottered to the left and gaped in amazement at the monster lying in the dust.

Silver Hair was motionless.

"It can't be," Nate mumbled, thinking the bear was playing possum. He swung the skull a final time and it shattered on impact, splitting down the middle and falling apart in his hands. The grizzly displayed no reaction.

Finally convinced Silver Hair was dead, Nate shuffled toward the ramp. His body was caked with sweat. Pain stabbed his chest with every step. Glancing down, he found five gashes where the bear's claws had ripped into him.

From on top of the bowl came the patter of rushing feet and the sound of heavy breathing, then a low growl.

Startled, thinking that Silver Hair must have a mate and it was about to tear into him, Nate looked up. At the upper edge of the ramp stood another huge animal, but this one was an enormous black dog, not a grizzly. It rushed down the incline and right up to him, then reared as it whined in delight.

"No!" Nate said, trying to brush the mongrel aside. In its enthusiasm the dog paid no heed and its heavy paws smacked into his chest, causing him to stumble backwards and fall onto his posterior. He sat there, a lopsided grin curling his mouth, as the black dog stepped up and began licking his face, getting slobber all over his cheeks and chin. "You dumb cur," he muttered.

"Samson, you found him!"

At the youthful cry of joy, Nate again looked up, and was astonished to see his son running toward him. "Zach?" he said in disbelief, trying to rise but unable to do so because Samson was straddling his legs.

"Pa! Pa!" the boy shouted. "You're alive!"

Nate could only sit in dumbfounded amazement as Zach threw himself into his arms and hugged him tight.

"I was so scared the Bloods had killed you," Zach said in a strained tone. "Ma kept saying you could take care of yourself, but I was scared anyway."

"Your mother?" Nate said, and suddenly spied Winona jogging along the rim. She wasn't alone. Trailing her were Touch the Clouds and Drags the Rope, both armed with bows.

Zach straightened, his eyes brimming with tears. "We had to come, Pa. Samson won't listen to anyone else but us, and we needed him to follow your scent. Touch the Clouds said we could find you faster using Samson than we could if the warriors had to follow the tracks the Bloods left."

Nate absently nodded. "True," he mumbled, and got to his knees. Zach stepped close for another hug.

"I love you, Pa," the boy said softly.

Feeling constricted in his throat, Nate embraced his son and silently gave thanks for being alive. To his rear, Samson began snarling. He twisted and saw the dog warily sniffing at the dead grizzly, the hairs on Samson's neck bristling. As he faced front a pair of slender arms circled Zach and him and warm lips touched his brow.

"You had me very worried, husband," Winona said huskily.

"I was worried also," Nate responded with a grin. There were tears of joy in her eyes as well. She pressed her face to his shoulder and gave a squeeze.

A shadow fell over all three of them. Touch the Clouds was beaming as he spoke. "My heart is happy to find you alive, Grizzly Killer. When we learned you were missing, I was sure some Blood would have your hair decorating his lodge before too many sleeps went by. It is good to see you are still wearing it."

Reverting to the Shoshone tongue, Nate asked, "What about the Blood war party?"

"All dead," stated Drags the Rope, stepping into view. "We saw them running toward us and ambushed them among the boulders. They were so busy looking back over their shoulders that they never saw us." He paused. "Most strange."

"Just the two of you killed all of them?"

"There are ten more men with us," Drags the Rope revealed. "They are still stripping the Bloods and dividing the spoils. We came on ahead with Winona."

"I can never repay you," Nate said, glancing from one warrior to the other. "I will always be in your debt."

The giant shifted self-consciously. "We are brothers in the same tribe, are we not? We only did what was right to do, the same as would you if one of us had been taken."

"Maybe so," Nate said, "but if either of you are ever in need, you have only to come to me and I will do all in my power to help you."

Winona and Zach straightened and moved back, and only then did they all notice the deep cuts where the bear had slashed him. "You've been hurt," she stated in concern.

"It's nothing," Nate said, rising slowly, his legs threatening to buckle. "A few scratches, nothing more."

Touch the Clouds was gazing at Silver Hair in frank awe. "Let me guess. *You* killed it?"

"Old age did more than I did."

"Our people will be telling tales of your exploits for as long as the sun rules the sky," Touch the Clouds said, and sighed. "It is just my luck to be living at the same time as you. No matter how many coup I count, you will be the one future generations remember."

"As a killer of bears perhaps," Nate said, dutifully returning the compliment. "But when it comes to glory in battle, I believe your name will be talked about around Shoshone camp fires more than any warrior in our history." He moved toward the incline, grimacing at an acute pang in his right side.

"What about this silver bear?" Drags the Rope asked. "Do you plan to take the hide back?"

"All I want is to lie down in my lodge and not move for a week," Nate replied. "I do not care if I ever see another bear, dead or alive, for as long as I live."

"But you must take the hide with you," Touch the Clouds protested, nodding at Silver Hair. "You killed this great beast. Our people must be permitted to see its huge skin and to hear from your own lips how you defeated such a formidable creature. It is your duty as a warrior to so honor yourself and our tribe."

Nate knew it was customary for warriors to publicly relate their exploits, but he was too tired and too sore to care about anything other than rest and recuperation. Wiping his sleeve across his forehead, he turned and spotted the rest of the Shoshone band making their way toward the ramp.

"If you are weary, we will skin the bear ourselves," Drags the Rope offered. "Such a fine hide will bring much good medicine to its owner and to our people."

"Whatever you wish," Nate said in resignation. It was useless to quibble, not to mention rude after they had risked their lives to save his. He sat down at the bottom of the ramp and rested his chin in his hands. The moment he did, Samson came over and resumed giving his face a saliva bath.

"We brought a water skin," Winona informed him. "I

will get it and tend your wounds. You stay here."

"I'm not going anywhere," Nate said, and tried to move his head away from his dog's drooling tongue, but Samson stepped closer and kept licking. Saliva dribbled down both cheeks and over his chin.

"Is there anything I can do, Pa?" Zach asked in English.

"As a matter of fact, there is," Nate said solemnly. "You can tie Samson's mouth shut for me."

His son, thinking he was joking, threw back his head and laughed.

Chapter Twelve

The entire village came out to meet them.

Nate walked at the rear of the band with his wife and son. Thanks to Winona's tender ministrations, he felt well again. She had applied an herbal poultice to the cuts on his chest and they no longer stung. His side still ached once in a while, but the pain was bearable. Considering the ordeal he had been through, he was in fine shape.

His weapons had been returned, and he felt like a whole man again with his knife, tomahawk, twin flintlocks, and rifle at his disposal. The Shoshones had offered him a share of the spoils taken from the dead Bloods, but he had refused and told them to divide everything, including the scalps, as they saw fit.

In front of him were two warriors carrying Silver Hair's hide. The size of three ordinary bear pelts, it wasn't so much heavy as it was awkward for a single person to tote. The warriors were quite excited about the trophy and couldn't wait to show it off to the tribe.

Now they got their chance.

From all directions the men, women, and children of the village swarmed toward the band. The return of a successful war party—in this case a rescue party—was always a cause for celebration. There would be plenty of food and drink and dancing later that night, and the warriors who took part in the rescue would regale their rapt listeners with their escapades.

Nate found himself surrounded by curious friends and relatives, all wanting to know what had happened. When it was learned he had killed a great silver bear, every last Shoshone wanted to hear the tale from his own lips. He promised all of them he would relate the full story that night.

Although he would rather have mingled and chatted, he was eager to get to his lodge and see how Reverend John Burke was faring. Since the band had camped overnight in the forest adjacent to the bald mountain to give him a chance to rest, not starting for the village until shortly after daylight, the minister had been left to his own devices for nearly two days. He hoped Burke had done nothing to antagonize the Shoshones.

As he hurried along with Winona on his right, Zach on his left, and Samson trotting behind him, he was stunned to see another white man come around a lodge, a grizzled mountain man sporting shoulder-length hair, a beard, and a mustache, all as white as the mantle of snow capping some of the distant peaks. So stunned was Nate that, halting in midstride, he almost tripped over his own feet.

"How now, Horatio!" the old-timer declared, his lake-blue eyes twinkling. "You tremble and look pale. Is not this something more than fantasy? What think you on it?"

"Shakespeare!" Nate blurted out, running forward to clasp his best friend by the shoulders. "We haven't seen you for months. What happened? Did Blue Water Woman get tired of your griping and boot you out of your cabin?''

Shakespeare McNair stiffened in mock indignation. ''My wife, I'll have you know, worships the ground I walk on. She would no more kick me out of the house than your lovely missus would you.''

''I've been tempted many times,'' Winona said, joining them and giving McNair a light peck on his bewhiskered cheek.

''Uncle Shakespeare!'' Zach chimed in. ''Are you going to stay a while? I want to show you how well I can ride a horse.''

''I might be so inclined,'' Shakespeare responded. ''If you're pa can tolerate my snoring for a few days.''

''I'll stick wax in my ears,'' Nate quipped, thrilled at this turn of events. Next to his wife and son, here was the man he loved most in the world, the man who had taught him practically everything he knew about the wilderness, the man who was a legend among the trappers and Indians alike. McNair, who had been dubbed Shakespeare years ago because of his fondness for the Bard of Avon and his penchant for quoting the playwright at the drop of a hat, had lived in the Rocky Mountains longer than any white man alive. He knew every trail, every pass. He knew the habits of every animal. He knew where to find rare medicinal plants few others were aware existed. McNair was a living fount of knowledge and no white man was more widely respected by the various tribes.

Shakespeare adopted a serious expression. ''Actually, son, this isn't strictly a pleasure call. I had a reason for coming to see you. I needed your help. Little did I know I'd find what I was looking for right here in the village. In fact, in your very lodge.''

''I don't understand,'' Nate said.

''Let's talk as we walk,'' McNair suggested, and slid between Winona and Nate as they all started off. ''I should fill you in before we get to your lodge so you know what's going on.'' He ran his fingers through his long beard. ''Now let's see. It was about a week and a half ago that some Flatheads showed up at my cabin. They were all kin to Blue Water Woman, and they'd found themselves a stray white man. A city man, no less.''

''You're not joshing me?''

Shakespeare shook his head. ''Seems they came on this gent wandering around the prairie near their village. He was as lost as could be. Thank goodness he stumbled on them first and not the Blackfeet.'' He idly surveyed the encampment. ''As you know, I've lived among the Flatheads and taught a few of them our language, so they were able to question this white man and learn what he was doing in their country. It turns out he was looking for someone and he wanted the Flatheads to help him. But they had a better idea.''

''They brought him to you,'' Nate deduced.

The mountain man nodded. ''Sure enough. They figured that since I know most everyone in these parts, I'd be the one who could help this man out. Well, I knew I'd need some help so naturally I thought of you. Got here just a few hours ago and heard all about you being captured by the Bloods.'' He glanced at Nate and made a clucking noise. ''Here I thought I taught you how to take care of yourself! If the word gets out, I'll be afraid to hold my head up in public.''

''As I recollect, *you* got yourself caught by the Blackfeet a few years ago. I was just following your example.''

McNair chuckled. ''True enough,'' he said, then quoted from his namesake. ''Thus far our fortune keeps an upward course, and we are graced with wreaths of victory. But, in the midst of this bright-shining day, I spy a black, suspicious threatening cloud, that will encounter with our glorious sun, ere he attain his easeful western bed.''

''I don't follow you,'' Nate admitted.

''What do you think of the Reverend John Burke?''

"You've met him?"

"No. Answer the question."

"He's a man with a chip on his shoulder the size of Long's Peak," Nate replied. "He wants to teach the Indians about Christianity, but with his attitude all he'll do is get them riled up."

"Then I was told the truth," Shakespeare said, frowning. "Unfeeling fools can with such wrongs dispense. I know his eye doth homage otherwhere; or else what lets it but he would be here?"

"Would you stop quoting that long-winded cuss and speak plain English?"

Shakespeare halted and touched his palm to his chest as if shocked. "Old William S. long-winded? Why, that's near blasphemy in my book. His too," he said, and cackled merrily.

"Will you get to the point?"

"The impatience of youth," Shakespeare said mockingly. "Very well. The lost gentleman's name is George Burke."

"He's related to the minister?"

"They're brothers."

Nate gazed straight ahead but had yet to catch a glimpse of his lodge. "Reverend Burke never even mentioned he had one. Were they traveling together and they became separated?"

"No," Shakespeare replied. "The good reverend left St. Louis alone. Then George, who is the younger of the two, cut out after him to try and stop him from doing what he intends to do."

"Which is?"

"You won't believe it."

"Tell me," Nate said a tad gruffly, wishing his mentor would come right out and say it instead of drawing out the suspense. But that was McNair. The man loved to gab. And while such a trait was highly entertaining on those

long nights when they were seated around a lonely camp-
fire off in the remote wilds, at other times it could be
downright aggravating.

Shakespeare looked Nate in the eyes. "Reverend Burke
plans to try and convert the Blackfeet to Christianity."

Both Nate and Winona halted in astonishment.

"I felt the same way when I first heard the news,"
McNair said.

Of all the tribes west of the Mississippi River, the Blackfeet were the most warlike, the most bloodthirsty. Ever
since an incident involving the Lewis and Clark expedition, when a Blackfoot warrior was slain and another
gravely wounded while trying to steal rifles belonging to
Meriwether Lewis and a few of his companions, the Blackfeet had viewed all whites with an implacable hatred. Trappers caught in their territory were tortured, killed, and
scalped. Every mountaineer, even greenhorns, knew to
stay away from the Blackfeet at all costs.

"There must be an explanation," Nate declared as he
walked forward. "Maybe the reverend doesn't realize how
dangerous the Blackfeet are."

"He knows," Shakespeare said. "George told me they
had a nasty argument in St. Louis over John's plan.
Despite all of George's protests, John refused to change
his mind."

Nate spied his lodge. And standing in front of it were
two men involved in a heated exchange. One was Reverend
Burke, the other a husky man with brown hair. That they
were brothers was self-evident; their facial features were
remarkably similar. As he drew closer he overheard their
dispute.

"... should never have come after me," the minister
was saying. "I didn't ask you to. I'm perfectly capable
of taking care of myself. Besides, the Lord will never let
any true harm befall me."

"You're not our Savior, you know."

"Meaning what?"

"That you can't perform miracles. The Blackfeet will laugh in your face, then carve you into little pieces. I'm not making this up. I've talked with men who know all about them."

"The Blackfeet may be heathens, but they are also children of God and deserve to hear the good news of the Gospel. Mark my words, George. One day there will be men of the cloth ministering to all these tribes."

George Burke shook his head in exasperation, then encompassed the village with a sweep of his arm. "Why not begin your ministry to the Indians here, among the Shoshones? At least *they* are friendly."

"I have made up my mind. I'm going to bring the Blackfeet to an acceptance of the Lord God and Our Master, Jesus Christ."

"Damn you, John!" George snapped, and whirled to stalk off. As it happened, he turned toward Nate and his family, and at the sight of them and McNair he hurried to greet them, his face a mask of barely suppressed fury. "You must be Nathaniel King," he said as he offered his right hand.

"My pleasure, Mr. Burke," Nate responded, shaking. He introduced Winona and Zach. "We couldn't help but overhear," he mentioned, nodding toward the lodge where Reverend Burke still stood.

George glanced at his brother and scowled. "John has become a fool. He'll get himself butchered and there is nothing I can do to stop him."

"You came all this way just to try and stop him from entering Blackfoot country?" Nate inquired.

The younger Burke nodded. "I tried to stop him in St. Louis, but he slipped out of the city in the middle of the night. By the time I bought my supplies and pack animals and took off after him, he had almost a two-day start." His voice lowered. "I love him dearly, but what is a man to do when his own flesh and blood is driven to commit suicide?''

Nate had no answer for that.

''If you'll excuse me,'' George said, his voice breaking, ''I need to walk alone awhile. I'll stop by in an hour or so, if that's all right with you?''

''We'll be expecting you.''

With a curt nod, George headed south, his head bowed, his fists clenched.

''Why are these men so upset with each other if they're brothers?'' Zach asked. ''Don't you always say that a family should stick together through thick and thin? I know if I ever get a little brother, I'll never get mad at him.''

Shakespeare chuckled and put his hand on Zach's head. ''Suggest but truth to my divining thoughts,'' he quoted. ''This pretty lad will prove our country's bliss. His looks are full of peaceful majesty, his head by nature framed to wear a crown, his hand to wield a sceptre, and himself likely in time to bless a regal throne.''

''Huh?'' Zach said.

''Pay no attention to Uncle Shakespeare,'' Nate advised. ''He's doing his best to confuse everyone today.'' Hefting the Hawken, he strode up to the minister. ''I take it you're feeling much better.''

''I was until my brother showed up,'' Burke replied. ''Now I'll have him pestering me until I ride out.'' He squinted up at the sun. ''It's too late in the day to leave now. We can depart tomorrow at first light if you're up to it.''

''We?''

''Yes. I need a reliable guide. From what your friend McNair was telling me, you're one of the most respected trappers in these mountains. I feared the Bloods had killed you, but your presence here proves you have courage. So at dawn we'll be on our way.''

"And just where do you expect me to guide you?"

"I imagine you know where. Into Blackfoot country, of course.''

Chapter Thirteen

Few words were spoken during the evening meal.

Winona served up a delicious elk stew, courtesy of her aunt, who provided the meat. She also made tasty cakes to dip in the stew and a boiled flour pudding for desert. Hot coffee capped off the supper.

Nate ate in somber silence. Normally, meals were an occasion for conversation and laughter, but the two brothers had put a damper on this one. John and George Burke sat across from each another, John the perfect picture of resentment and George wearing his anger on his sleeve. Their attitudes affected even young Zach, who usually talked incessantly; this evening he ate quietly, occasionally giving the two men a timid quizzical glance.

When the meal was over and Winona was busily clearing away the tin pans and flat pieces of bark that had been used as plates, Nate shifted to adjust his crossed legs and regarded the brothers coldly. ''I think it's time we cleared the air and settled a few things. Your personal affairs are none of my business, but since the reverend has asked me to help him, I have a right to speak my piece."

"What's your decision?" John Burke asked.

Nate raised his tin cup to his lips and swallowed a mouthful of coffee. He had put off the minister earlier by informing the older Burke he needed time to decide whether he would serve as an escort to Blackfoot territory. In reality he had wanted the time to think up a way to convince John Burke he was making the biggest mistake of his life.

"Well?" the reverend prompted impatiently.

"I've given the matter a great deal of thought," Nate said. "And I have to be honest. I agree with your brother."

Reverend Burke glowered, placed his hands on the ground, and began to rise. "I should have known."

"Wait," Nate said. "Hear me out."

"There is nothing you can say that will persuade me to change my mind," the minister responded, although he relaxed his arms and leaned back. "But out of courtesy I will listen to whatever it is."

Nate glanced at Shakespeare, who was filling a pipe and appeared distinctly uninterested in the entire matter, then at the brothers. "If it was practically any other tribe, Reverend, I would take you to them without hesitation. The Nez Percé, the Flatheads, the Bannocks, the Sioux, they are all reasonably friendly to whites. They would hear you out, and they'd allow you to leave in peace whenever you wanted." He tapped his coffee cup with a forefinger. "The Blackfeet will kill you before you can open your mouth."

"You can't be certain of that."

"But I can. More white men have lost their lives to the Blackfeet than to all the other tribes combined. You will be dead five minutes after you run into them unless they're of a mind to torture you first to see how brave you are. In that case you'll live a bit longer."

"The Lord is my rock, and my fortress, and my deliverer; my God, my strength in whom I trust, my buckler, and the horn of my salvation, and my high tower," Burke said, quoting Scripture. "I have nothing to fear."

Nate tried another argument. "All right then. Let's suppose you do meet up with the Blackfeet. How will you teach them about God and Jesus when none of them, to my knowledge, speak English? Do you know sign language?"

"No."

"Do you know the Blackfoot tongue?"

"Of course not."

"Then how will you teach them?"

"Where there is a will, there is a way," Reverend Burke said. "I trust in the Lord. He will guide me."

"If you don't mind my saying so, I don't think you're being very realistic," Nate commented.

"I do mind," Reverend Burke stated, and stood. "Thank you for an excellent meal, Mrs. King. And I want to thank both of you for the gracious hospitality you've shown me. You'll be glad to hear that I won't be a burden to you much longer." Wheeling, he stepped to the flap.

"Wait," Nate said, but the minister paid no heed. The flap closed and John Burke was gone.

"He will never listen to reason," George said bitterly. "My brother is the world's biggest fool."

Shakespeare, who until that moment had been uncommonly reticent, not uttering so much as a syllable, now grunted and said, "All places that the eye of heaven visits are to a wise man ports and happy havens. Teach thy necessity to reason thus; there is no virtue like necessity."

George gave the mountain man a sharp look. "Are you saying you agree with his insanity?"

"Not at all," Shakespeare said. "I merely made an

observation written years ago by old William S."

"Explain what you meant. I don't follow you."

"No one ever does," Nate joked, leaning forward. He cradled the coffee cup in his hands and swirled the dark brew a few times. "George, what will John do now that I've turned him down? Will he give up and go back to St. Louis?"

"Never. Not him. He's too pigheaded."

"But without a guide his chances of finding a Blackfoot village are slim."

"That won't stop him," George said, his shoulders sagging. "You see, there's more to this notion of his than you know."

"Enlighten us," Shakespeare said.

The younger Burke sighed, his brow furrowed in deep contemplation. After a while he glanced at them and bobbed his chin. "Very well. By all rights John should be telling you this, but he won't ever tell a soul." He ran a hand through his hair. "You see, my brother wasn't always as stubborn as he is today. Once he was the kindest, most tolerant man you would ever want to meet. He tried his utmost to live the Golden Rule, to love everyone, to do unto others as he would have them do to him. He was highly respected and his church services were usually filled to overflowing."

Outside arose a few shouts and loud laughter. The Shoshones were gathering for the night's festivities.

"John had a lovely wife named Pearl," George went on, "and they were the proud parents of a six-year-old boy they named Solomon. They were loving, caring parents. You would have marveled to see them."

"It hardly sounds like the same man," Nate said.

"True," George said sadly. "And with good reason." He inhaled loudly. "Not quite a year ago John took his family from our hometown in Rhode Island to St. Louis. He'd heard about the rowdy, godless types who inhabit that city, and he figured there was a great spiritual need he could fill. Very few ministers venture anywhere near the frontier. He wanted to be one of the first.''

"Where are his wife and son now?" Nate asked.

"Bear with me," George said. "About six months after John began his new ministry, I received a letter from him. It turned out that the trappers, mountain men, and traders in his flock had filled his head with tales about the many Indian tribes living on the plains and in the mountains. And do you know what impressed him the most? The fact the Indians were all heathens. He saw an even greater need than in St. Louis. So earlier this year he started out with Pearl and Solomon for the Rockies.''

Shakespeare's head shot up. "All by themselves?''

"Yes. I wrote him and tried to convince him that he was putting his family at great risk, but he never answered me. After all the stories I had read in the newspapers about trappers and other travelers who had run-ins with the Indians, I was extremely worried. I suggested he find another party heading west and travel with them.'' George closed his eyes and touched a hand to his brow.

No comments were necessary. Nate solemnly waited for the younger Burke to continue, certain he knew how the account would end.

"The next thing, about a month and a half after my brother departed St. Louis, I received a letter from a man who was a former member of my brother's congregation there. It turned out that John had been back for two or three weeks and never let me know. The man kindly told me there had been a terrible tragedy, that both Pearl and Solomon had been slain. John was distraught, and the man felt I might be able to comfort him. So I left immediately for St. Louis.''

All eyes were on George as he took a hasty sip of coffee.

"I found him easily enough, and I couldn't believe the

change that had come over him. He wasn't the brother I remembered. His whole personality was different. Where before he had been kind and considerate, now he was bitter and rude. And nothing I said or did would bring him around.''

"What happened to his family, sir?" Zachary inquired.

George licked his lips. "They were killed by Indians. John refused to talk about it, but I was able to find the three trappers who had found him and brought him all the way back to St. Louis. They told me John and his family camped in a stand of trees beside a small stream. Apparently, a band of Indians spotted them and that night closed in. John was at the stream, bending down to fill a bucket with water when he was hit over the head, struck from behind with a tomahawk. The Indians must have figured they'd split his skull because they left him there and went after Pearl and Solomon.''

"You don't need to finish," Nate said softly. "We can guess what happened.''

"No, I don't mind," George said. "You might as well know. It will help you to understand why my brother is acting the way he is.'' He took another deep breath. "From the tracks at the scene, the trappers believed Solomon had tried to go to John's aid and was stabbed in the chest, then scalped. Pearl was stripped naked, ravaged, and had her throat slit. They probably would have scalped John too, but they must have seen the trappers approaching the camp fire and left.''

In the profound silence that ensued, the laughter and happy voices of the Shoshones outside seemed grossly inappropriate.

"Did the trappers know which tribe was responsible?" Shakespeare asked.

George shook his head. "They scoured the area but all they found were a few moccasin prints and hoof tracks. The Indians didn't leave any solid clues behind.'' He coughed. "The oldest trapper thought a band of Kiowas might have done the deed based on the stitching of the moccasins."

Nate frowned. It was indeed possible to note the stitching pattern if a footprint was left in soft soil, such as at the edge of a stream. And the Kiowas, while not as widely feared as the Blackfeet, were formidably ruthless in their own right and prone to exterminating any whites they encountered.

"John was beside himself when the trappers revived him. He refused to eat for days and came near dying himself. By the time they reached St. Louis he was a skeleton. He's still thinner than he ever was in his whole life. I doubt he eats regularly. His guilt is gnawing away at his soul, and if he keeps on as he's doing he'll eventually waste away to nothing." George paused. "But he doesn't intend to let it get that far."

"No," Shakespeare said, and launched into another quote. "Methink I am a prophet new inspired and thus expiring do foretell of him: His rash fierce blaze of riot cannot last, for violent fires soon burn out themselves; small showers last long, but sudden storms are short; he tires betimes that spurs too fast betimes; with eager feeding food doth choke the feeder: Light vanity, insatiate cormorant, consuming means, soon preys upon itself."

"When did he get this crazy notion of ministering to the Blackfeet?" Nate inquired.

"About six or seven weeks ago, when he was talking to the same trappers who had saved him. They told him that converting the Indians was impossible, that his heart had been in the right place but he was wrong in thinking the Indians would be remotely interested in the white man's religion. I was there. I saw the look on his face when the oldest trapper mentioned that some tribes were decent while others were devils incarnate."

"And this trapper mentioned the Blackfeet by name," Shakespeare said.

"Yes. He went on about them at length, how they are the worst of the lot, fiends who delight in inflicting pain and seeing others suffer."

Nate shared a melancholy look with Winona. They both understood John Burke now. Nate, in particular, could identify with how the minister must be feeling. Should anything ever happen to his wife or Zach he would probably react in the same way.

"I had no intention of becoming involved in this," Shakespeare said. "But now I guess it's my duty to sit down with your brother, George, and explain the facts of frontier existence to him."

George mustered a wan smile. "I appreciate the offer but it won't do any good. John has his mind made up. Nothing we can do will change it."

"With time maybe we can change it," Nate said confidently. "And we'll buy that time by taking his horses and supplies over to Touch the Cloud's lodge and asking Touch the Clouds to keep them there until we fetch them. John can't go anywhere on foot and without provisions. If we do our best, in three or four days he might see reason."

"I don't know," George said uncertainly.

"What have we got to lose?" Nate responded. "Touch the Clouds will be busy at the celebration tonight, so first thing in the morning, before your brother wakes up, I'll sneak everything over. John will have no choice but to hear us all out if he wants to get his effects back."

"I suppose you're right," George said. "But you don't know my brother like I do. When he sets his mind to something, watch out. If there's a way to foil us, he'll think of it."

"Relax. Everything will be fine," Nate assured him.

"For the time being let's enjoy the celebration and forget all about it."

Not twelve hours later he was to deeply regret those words.

Chapter Fourteen

Dimly Nate became aware of a hand roughly shaking his right shoulder. He instantly sat bolt upright, blinking to focus while trying to clear lingering tendrils of sleep from his mind. The interior of the lodge was dark except for burning embers in the fire. The acrid scent of smoke tingled his nostrils. To his right lay Winona, sound asleep. Also asleep were Zach and George Burke. Beside him squatted Shakespeare wearing a pensive expression.

"Sorry to wake you," McNair whispered, "but I figured you should know that the minister is gone."

"Gone?" Nate repeated, and again gazed around the lodge. "Maybe he's out watering the grass."

"What do you think I was just doing?" Shakespeare said. "That's when I noticed his horses were missing. So are all of his supplies."

Suddenly Nate was completely awake. He rose and glanced at the vacant spot where John Burke's provisions had been piled. "Damn," he muttered, hastening outdoors. A faint pink tinge lined the eastern horizon, signifying dawn was an hour or so off. Dashing around to the rear of the lodge, he saw Pegasus and his other animals, Shakespeare's white mare, and the two horses belonging to George Burke. Nowhere was there any sign of the minister's bay and pair of pack animals.

"I figure the reverend skunked us but good," Shakespeare said at his elbow. "He lit out last night while all of us were at the celebration."

Nate turned. Could it be true? Come to think of it, he didn't recall seeing John at the festivities, nor had he seen him when they all returned to the lodge shortly after midnight. He hadn't thought much of it at the time, assuming John was still mad at George and had gone off somewhere to pray or simply to be by himself.

"Either he overheard our talk about taking his horses and supplies, or he just wanted to put as much distance as he could between his brother and him so George couldn't stop him from riding into Blackfoot country," Shakespeare speculated.

"We have to go after him," Nate declared, staring at the eastern sky. If they left at first light they might be able to overtake the reverend by noon.

"We might be wasting our time," Shakespeare said. "What if we catch up with him and he doesn't want to come back? Do we truss him up and haul him back here anyway?"

Nate shrugged. "We'll cross that bridge when we come to it. All I know is we can't let him go off and kill himself. He's throwing his life away for nothing."

"Maybe he doesn't see it that way."

"I'll never be able to live with myself if we don't try," Nate said, and hastened inside.

George Burke was propped on his elbows. "What's going on?" he asked with a yawn. "I saw Shakespeare and you whispering, then you both ran outside. Is something wrong?"

Nate would much rather go in pursuit with only Shakespeare at his side. George was a greenhorn who knew next to nothing about wilderness survival and inevitably would slow then down. But George was the minister's kin, and as such Nate had no right to refuse him. "Your brother has run off."

"What?" George exclaimed loud enough to rouse a bear from hibernation, and came off his blanket as if he'd been shot from a cannon. "When?"

"We think he left last night sometime before we got back," Nate disclosed, shifting to see both Winona and Zach now awake and sitting up.

"Then we must go after him right away," George declared, stooping to grab his boots. "We can't let him reach Blackfoot territory."

"I know," Nate said, "but we can't go off half-cocked either. We'll have breakfast, pack some jerky and whatever else we'll require on the trail, and ride out as soon as the sun rises. We'll need the light to follow his tracks."

"All right," George said sourly. "You know best."

I thought I did, Nate thought to himself, and went over to his loved ones.

A few tiny clouds, like balls of cotton adrift in an azure sea, were the only things moving in the morning sky when Nate, Shakespeare, and George Burke rode out of the Shoshone village, heading to the northeast. Nate had asked Winona's aunt and her husband to keep an eye on his family while he was gone. Spotted Bull, Touch the Clouds, and Drags the Rope had all offered to help, but Nate had declined their generosity.

This was his problem. Since he had been the one who brought Reverend Burke to the village, and since his lapse in judgment had enabled the minister to get such a substantial head start, he felt directly responsible for John Burke's welfare. In addition, he was annoyed at himself for not taking the man's horses and supplies over to Touch the Clouds before leaving for the celebration. If he had, Burke could never have given them the slip.

They found the tracks left by the minister's three animals right away. Reverend Burke had hugged the shore of the lake, leaving clear prints the whole time, until he reached the north end, at which point he turned into the forest.

Shakespeare leaned down to study the trail. "He was moving fast," he remarked.

"Can he elude us?" George asked.

"Not in a million years. He's leading two packhorses while we have our grub in our parfleches," Nate said, giving the rawhide pouches draped behind his saddle a pat. Parfleches were the Indian equivalent of saddlebags, and his were crammed with enough jerked venison and pemmican to last him two weeks. "We can go faster than he can. It's only a matter of time until we overtake him."

"I hope you're right," George said.

For the next ten miles they traversed dense woodland. Then the tracks slanted almost due east for a mile along a winding valley before turning to the northeast once more. Minutes later they found themselves at the top of a bald hill.

"He stopped here for a bit," Shakespeare noted as he read the hoofprints.

"Why?" George wondered.

"He was getting his bearings," Nate said. "My guess is he hoped to spot the prairie from here but he wasn't quite close enough yet."

George gazed eastward at the sprawling vista of tree-covered foothills. "What significance does the prairie hold?"

"He can make better time on the plains and spot others coming a long way off. Too, he probably knows the Blackfeet have their villages on the plains to the east of the Rockies, but north of here. All he has to do is continue north and in a week or so he'll be in the middle of their country.''

''If he doesn't run into one of their roving war parties before that, or something worse,'' Shakespeare said.

''What could be worse?'' George asked anxiously.

''All sorts of nasty fates await men who presume to tackle the wilderness on their own terms instead of learning Nature's habits and acting accordingly.''

''Is that more from William Shakespeare?''

McNair chuckled. ''Good Lord, no. That was original. But I know what I'm talking about, son. I've lived in the Rockies for more years than Nate and you have lived combined, and I know the dangers better than anyone.'' He clucked his white horse into motion and took the lead.

Nate fell in behind George Burke. Since Shakespeare was preoccupied with following the tracks, he had to keep alert for hostiles, grizzlies, and whatnot. One of them had to be on the watch at all times, or they might blunder into an ambush or a lurking bear.

In a way, they were lucky. Reverend Burke's pack animals were heavily burdened and left deep impressions. If Burke was on foot, tracking him would be impossible from horseback because they would need to get close to the ground to properly read the telltale smudges, crushed blades of grass, and partial prints that walking men made. That was why the Shoshones who came to his rescue had not used their horses; the Bloods had all been on foot.

Another hour brought them to a valley leading due north. Nate was puzzled when the trail led up it. If Reverend Burke was heading for the plains, as he surmised, then the tracks should continue on eastward. Why this new change of direction?

The air was crystal clear. A bald eagle glided high up, seeking prey. A marmot squatting beside its burrow near a cluster of boulders spotted them, vented a shrill whistle, and disappeared in a flash into the security of its den.

As always, Nate drank in the magnificent splendor of the untamed land. Shakespeare was of the opinion that one day, far in the future, the West would be just like the East: overrun with people, crowded with towns and cities, the wild creatures reduced to small populations or killed off completely. They had discussed this bleak outlook on several occasions, and Nate fervently hoped his mentor was wrong. To have the unspoiled wonder of the rolling prairie and the lofty Rockies reduced to mere stepping-stones on man's relentless trek to the Pacific was a travesty of progress and an affront against Nature. Why, if humankind kept on as they had been doing, one day the whole world would be filled to overflowing with more people than the planet could handle. What then? Where would the people of the future go to enjoy the natural beauty now so abundant once the wilderness was gone?

Movement in trees high on a foothill brought his reflection to an end and he squinted up at the pines. Shortly a large bull elk stepped into a clearing and gazed down at them. It was alone. Later in the year, during the mating season, the bull would congregate with others of its kind and battle other bulls for the attentions of the cows. Nate had witnessed the spectacle many times. The bulls would challenge one another with their distinctive bugling cries, then rush at each other, their racks clashing with a crash that could be heard a hundred yards away. Rarely was one killed. Those bulls that proved stronger gathered harems that would make a sheik of Arabia jealous, sometimes numbering 50 or more.

They came on a stream and halted to water their mounts. Shakespeare dismounted to squat and examine the ground. "The reverend stopped here too. Not long, though. He was still in a hurry."

"He knows I'll come after him," George said. "He's

counting on outrunning me.''

"Have you given some thought to what you'll do when we catch him?" Shakespeare asked.

"Not really," George answered. "I figure I'll try to talk him out of carrying through with this foolishness. What else can I do?"

"Tie him up and lug him back to the village."

"Bind my own brother? A man of the cloth?"

Shakespeare rose. "He's already proven he won't listen to reason. And I, for one, don't intend to sit around a camp fire close to Blackfoot territory for two or three days while you try to persuade him. It would be safer to take him back whether he wants to go or not."

George bit his lower lip. "I don't know if I could do that to my own flesh and blood."

"Your choice. Just bear in mind he won't have flesh or blood if the Blackfeet get ahold of him."

Soon they were on their way, riding to the end of the valley where the tracks headed up and over another foothill.

"He's scouring the country again," Nate commented when they were at the top.

From the hill, the minister had traveled due east, keeping to the low ground to make better time.

"Thank goodness he's not sticking to the high ground," Shakespeare remarked. "A man stands out like a sore thumb up there."

A small pond was their next stop. In the soil at the water's edge were the reverend's boot tracks and a single hand print where he had leaned down to drink.

"Your brother must not be feeling up to snuff," Shakespeare told George. "There's no need for him to be stopping to drink as often as he does."

"He's not fully recovered from what happened on the plains," George said. "If he's not careful he'll have a relapse."

"Could be," Shakespeare said, "and if he collapses out here with no one to tend him, he's in big trouble."

Reverend Burke, inexplicably, had borne to the northeast once he left the pond, into dense forest of large fir and spruce. They followed the hoof tracks, passing under trees in which squirrels scooted about and birds sang. Periodically frightened rabbits would bound from their path in prodigious leaps.

George twisted to see Nate. "Is it always like this, always so indescribably beautiful?"

"Always," Nate said.

"I think I understand why you stay in these mountains instead of going back to civilization," George said wistfully. "In the States there are a lot of people who believe men like McNair and you are crazy. Now I know better."

Nate gazed around and smiled. "It does grow on a man. I never planned on becoming a free trapper, but once I'd been out here a spell I knew I'd never be able to go back and live in the States again. Give me the wide open spaces and freedom over a crowded city and a hectic life any day."

The forest thinned out and they rode out onto a spacious meadow. They'd only gone a dozen yards when Shakespeare abruptly reined up and jumped down.

"What is it?" George asked.

"Your brother has company. Four Indians are following him now."

Chapter Fifteen

Nate was promptly at Shakespeare's side, bending low to read the spoor. Sure enough, he saw where four sets of hoofprints, all unshod horses, had come out of the woods and fallen into a line as they stalked Reverend Burke.

"What kind of Indians are they?" George inquired, his anxiety as plain as the nose on his face.

"Can't tell from the tracks," Nate replied. "They could be Bannocks who are just curious."

"Bannocks are friendly to whites?"

"Sometimes they are, sometimes they aren't. All depends on their mood at the time," Nate said, and when the younger Burke blanched he added as reassurance, "They have close ties with the Shoshones and some of their bands are just as friendly."

"What other tribes frequent this area?"

Nate rested the stock of the Hawken on the ground. "Oh, the Crows, Arapahos, even the Cheyennes."

"Don't forget the Blackfeet," Shakespeare interjected.

"But since they go about mostly on foot, these Indians are probably from one of the tribes you mentioned."

George gestured impatiently. "Let's quit wasting time. My brother could be at death's door as we speak."

"Don't get yourself in an uproar," Shakespeare cautioned, stepping to his mare. "Whoever these Indians are, they came on your brother's trail quite a spell after he went by. Their tracks are so fresh I'd guess they're not more than half an hour ahead of us."

"Then what are we waiting for?" George demanded, moving out ahead of them.

"Uh-oh," Shakespeare said softly as he swung up. "Here's Agamemnon, an honest fellow enough and one that loves quails; but he has not so much brain as earwax." He urged the mare into a gallop.

As before, Nate brought up the rear. He followed his companions and kept a constant eye on the surrounding hills. Miles to the west reared the first line of jagged peaks denoting the mountains proper, peaks glistening bright with snow. Miles to the east, but out of sight, lay the grass-carpeted prairie.

He hoped the four Indians were Crows. Like the Shoshones and the Nez Percé, the Crows were invariably friendly to whites. There had been an incident a few years ago at a Rendezvous when a couple of thoughtless trappers had gotten an old Crow drunk. An irate band of young warriors had threatened to beat the fools within an inch of their lives, and had only been dissuaded by trappers they respected. The Crows hated the white man's fool water, as they called distilled spirits of any kind. They believed that once a Crow drank liquor, he ceased to be a Crow and became a stupid animal. Trying to sell spirits to a Crow was as chancy as trying to feed raw meat to a panther.

An hour and a half went by. From the evidence presented by the tracks, the Indians made no attempt to narrow the gap between them and Reverend Burke, who stuck to valley after valley.

George pressed on ahead, able to follow the trail himself since the trampled grass and gouged earth was now so easy to read.

As they were passing a bluff on their right, Shakespeare called sternly, "You can slow down, son. Wearing out our horses will only delay us."

"I'm not slowing down until my brother is safe."

Shakespeare moved up beside him. "I wasn't asking you, George. As much as I share your concern, the horses come first. Do as I say or I'll make you walk."

Nate had opened his mouth to agree with McNair when he happened to glance at the bluff and detected a glint of sunlight at the top. The distance, close to two hundred yards, prevented him from seeing the cause. But he dared not ignore it. "Keep acting normally and don't look at the bluff," he warned the others. "There's someone up there."

"What did you see?" Shakespeare asked.

"Might have been sun on a rifle barrel."

Forgetting Nate's advice, George started to turn toward the bluff, but was stopped by a smack on the arm from Shakespeare.

"We don't want whoever it is to know we know he's watching us," the mountain man said.

"But what if it's a hostile and he takes it into his head to shoot at us?"

"We're a hundred and fifty yards off if we're a yard," Shakespeare responded. "He'd have to be a damn fine shot, and he knows that even if he bagged one of us the other two can reach the trees before he reloads and then go after him."

"There might be more than one," George argued, convinced they were in mortal jeopardy.

"We'll find out soon enough," Nate said. "I aim to ride up and have a look."

"We could all go," Shakespeare said.

"And make three times as much noise," Nate replied. "No, I'll go by myself. You know what to do."

"We'll be waiting," Shakespeare said, and grinned at him. "Shoot sharp's the word."

"What?" George asked.

"That's trapper lingo for good luck."

"Oh."

Waiting until the valley curved to the right and a projecting arm of pines blocked the bluff from view, Nate yanked on the reins and rode rapidly into the forest. Bending low over the saddle, the Hawken clutched in his left hand, he headed for the north base of the bluff. If whoever was up there was still watching, it would be a minute before Shakespeare and Burke rode into sight. By the time the person figured out Nate was no longer with them, he would be at the bluff.

Thick undergrowth enabled him to reach his goal without mishap. Straightening, he held Pegasus to a walk and moved eastward along the base. The front of the bluff consisted of a gently sloping hill covered with high grass, scattered pines, and infrequent boulders. He drew rein under a spruce to scan the hill carefully, and was rewarded by spying a ground-hitched, saddled roan halfway up the slope.

He moved toward it. A saddle meant a white man. Who did he know who might be roaming through this region? He could think of no one, and since it wasn't wise to ride right up to a man who might not want to be found, he dismounted next to the roan and grounded the stallion's reins. Then, his Hawken at the ready, he slowly climbed the hill.

The bluff leveled off near the top. Nate glided silently, his footfalls muffled by the grass underfoot, using all available cover, moving from boulder to tree to clump of weeds like a buckskin-clad ghost. He had learned his lessons well, and few were the warriors who could move more quietly.

Someone coughed above him and to the left.

Nate crouched, the grass swishing lightly against his moccasins as he advanced. There was a row of small boulders near the rim and a solitary stunted pine. Suddenly a shadow separated itself from the trunk and inched closer to the rim. His thumb on the hammer, Nate crept forward until behind one of the boulders. Tensing, he stood upright and trained his rifle on the figure squatting in the open. "Howdy, friend."

The man whirled, his face showing astonishment. A lanky frontiersman in typical buckskins and moccasins, he had oily black hair worn well past his shoulders and a greased mustache but no beard. His eyes were brown, his tanned skin the result of spending all his time in the outdoors. "Tarnation, mister!" he declared. "You plumb scared me half to death!"

Nate saw a telescope clutched in the man's right hand. So that explained the glint of sunlight he had seen. A sizeable number of mountaineers, including the redoubtable Jim Bridger, relied on telescopes when scouting the country around them. As Bridger had once joked in Nate's presence, "It's easier to give a band of hostiles out for scalps the slip when you see them coming a mile off than when they pop up out of a ravine right in front of you."

"Why'd you sneak up on me anyway?" the frontiersman demanded, regaining his composure.

"I like to know who's spying on me," Nate replied. "What's your name?"

"Allen. Henry Allen, from Tennessee. And who might you be?"

"Nate King. Some folks know me better as Grizzly Killer," Nate answered, stepping around the boulder and slowly lowering his Hawken. He noticed Allen's rifle propped against the stunted pine. Allen also had a belt knife and a single flintlock.

"I saw you at the last Rendezvous but never got a chance to talk to you. You're Shakespeare McNair's close friend, as I recollect."

"I am," Nate allowed, suppressing a smile. For all his fame as a killer of bears, Shakespeare had him beat hands down. McNair was a truly legendary figure among trappers and Indians alike, more widely recognized than Bridger himself.

"Was that him I saw you with down yonder?"

Nodding, Nate moved forward and offered his right hand. "I apologize for spooking you. But as you must know, a man doesn't live long out here by being careless."

Allen grinned. "Believe you me, I know. I've been trapping for pretty near two years."

"What are you doing in this neck of the woods?"

Allen closed his collapsible telescope, then gestured to the northwest. "I've been living with some Crows for the better part of ten months. Have me a Crow wife and a sprout on the way come fall." He stepped to the tree to reclaim his long rifle, a Kentucky in fine condition. "Their village is about four days' ride from here. My wife has been nagging me about needing a new buffalo robe, so I'm on my way to the plains. I stopped to rest my horse and while I was sitting up here keeping my eyes peeled for hostiles, who should I see but four Arapahos heading north."

"Arapahos?" Nate repeated, worried for the minister. Or more precisely, the minister's horses and possessions. Arapahos were not inherently warlike, as were the Blackfeet, but they would steal a man's belongings if they felt they could get away with it.

"Why are you so concerned?" Allen asked. "They went by forty minutes ago or more."

Briefly, Nate told Henry Allen about Reverend John Burke and the reverend's plan to try and convert the Blackfeet to Christianity.

"Is the man touched in the head?'

"In a sense," Nate said, sighing. He related the fate of John Burke's family.

"My. That's sure a pity," Allen said at the conclusion of the story. "A man of the cloth, no less. I guess it can happen to the best of us." He hefted his Kentucky. "Tell you what, friend. If you have no objections, I'd like to tag along and lend a hand. Some folks say I'm a fair shot, and I know this country hereabouts better than most because I hunt and trap it all the time."

"We'd be happy to have you," Nate said gratefully. When confronting Indians, there was always greater safety in numbers. Most warriors would think twice about tackling a superior force of whites, but wouldn't hesitate a second if they outnumbered their intended victims.

"Lead the way," Allen said, and when they had gone a few feet added, "I heard tell that you have a Shoshone wife and a young'un."

"I do."

"And that you kill grizzlies with a swat of your hand."

Nate laughed. "I wish it was so easy."

"Killed any lately?"

"Two within the past few days."

Allen broke stride, then quickly recovered. "Oh. Is that *all*? Maybe sometime you'll share the secret of your success. I for one go in the opposite direction when I see a grizzly coming."

"My secret is no mystery. It's called bad luck."

"How can killing grizzlies right and left be bad? Would you rather they killed *you*?"

"It's not the killing, it's running into the blamed things in the first place."

"Never thought of it that way."

Once on their mounts, Nate led his newfound acquaintance down to the base of the bluff and into the forest. Now if they could only overtake the Arapahos before the Arapahos overtook John Burke, they might be able to avert serious trouble. Speed was of the essence.

He found Shakespeare and George a quarter of a mile from the point where he had left them, waiting in the shade at the edge of the trees. Once introductions were over and Nate disclosed the identity of the four warriors, he assumed the lead and pressed Pegasus into a gallop. None of the others spoke; they all appreciated the gravity of the situation.

The reverend's trail took them on a winding course among the foothills instead of making for the prairie as Nate had guessed would be the case. Nate got the impression John Burke had been looking for something. But what? A place to camp? More water? Rounding a low hill, he suddenly reined up, his gaze fastened on a thin column of white smoke spiraling skyward half a mile distant.

"My brother has stopped!" George exclaimed, and raced ahead, lashing his steed with the ends of his reins.

"Hold up!" Nate cried, but was ignored. He gave chase, seeking some sign of the Arapahos, afraid George would recklessly rush into an ambush. To his rear thundered Shakespeare's and Allen's horses. They covered a quarter of a mile before Nate was able to draw abreast of George. "Slow down!" he bellowed. "You're putting all our lives at risk."

"My brother might need us! I'm not halting until we're there!"

"Yes, you are," Nate retorted angrily. Lunging to the right, he grabbed George's reins and wrenched them from the unsuspecting man's grasp, forcing George to grab onto his saddle and cling to it to keep from being spilled onto the ground. Nate brought Pegasus and Burke's animal to a gradual stop, and was about to give George a tongue-lashing when from the vicinity of the smoke arose a series of shrill war whoops.

Chapter Sixteen

"Damn!" Nate snapped, flinging George's reins down. Digging his heels into Pegasus, he flew toward the smoke, the fringe on his buckskins flapping in the wind. Reverend Burke had made camp in a stand of firs through which a narrow creek flowed. Until Nate reached the trees, he couldn't see what was happening. But as he dove in among the trunks he glimpsed a number of horses on the east bank and several figures moving about near a fire.

His arrival took the Arapahos by surprise. They were in the act of plundering the minister's supplies, whooping and venting cries of delight at their finds, and consequently didn't hear him coming until he was among them. He burst from cover into the clearing in which the camp was situated just as a tall warrior held aloft a spare pair of long underwear and crowed loudly.

Three of the band were by the crackling fire, the fourth standing near the prone form of Reverend Burke. They all spun, and the tall one dropped the long underwear and grabbed for a tomahawk at his waist.

Nate reined up with one hand as he jammed the Hawken to his shoulder with the other and trained the barrel on the tall warrior. The Arapaho recoiled backwards anticipating a ball in the chest. But Nate held his fire. His meaning was clear. If any of them pulled a weapon on him, he would shoot.

For a moment the outcome hung in the balance, the warriors frozen in indecision, Nate doing his best to keep the Hawken trained on the tall Arapaho despite the fidgeting of his stallion. And then Shakespeare, Allen, and George arrived, the first two with their rifles leveled.

The younger Burke took one look at his brother and leaped to the ground. He started to run over when a harsh command from Nate halted him in his tracks.

"Not yet! Don't get between us and these Indians or you might be caught in the cross fire if they decide to put up a fight!"

"But John—"

"Will have to wait," Nate ordered. He slid off of Pegasus and warily approached the tall warrior, lowering his Hawken to waist height but kept the man covered. "Do you speak their tongue, Shakespeare?" he asked without taking his eyes off the Arapaho. So far as he knew, his friend was fluent in four Indian languages, spoke three others passably well, and might know more. McNair wasn't the type to brag about his accomplishments.

"Can't say as I do," Shakespeare answered. "Always wanted to but somehow or other I never got around to it. Once I hit seventy I started to slow down. No excuse for it other than outright laziness, I reckon."

"Watch them like a hawk," Nate cautioned, and tucked the Hawken under his left arm to free his hands. "I am Grizzly Killer of the Shoshone," he signed, then pointed at the minister. "This man is my friend. Have you killed him?"

"I am Running Antelope of the Arapaho," the tall war-rior responded. "Do not blame me or my friends for his condition."

"Then why is he lying there?"

Running Antelope glanced up at Shakespeare, then at Shakespeare's rifle. "I do not know. We were following him, waiting for a chance to steal his horses, when he made his camp at this spot. We watched him build his fire, walk to the stream, and drink some water. As he moved toward his horses he suddenly put a hand to his forehead and fell. We did not touch him."

Nate believed him. While Arapahos might be horse thieves and occasionally cold-hearted killers, they were no worse in their dealings with whites than any other tribe, not counting the Blackfeet and their confederates. And the Arapahos certainly weren't liars. Few warriors in any of the tribes made lying a regular practice because of the scorn that would be heaped on them if they were caught. By and large, Indians in general were much more honest than their white counterparts.

He sidled over to the minister and dropped to one knee to touch his hand to John Burke's cheek. It was as hot as the nearby fire. Pressing his palm to Burke's brow con-firmed the reverend was burning up with fever.

"Is he—?" George asked, unable to finish the question.

"He's alive," Nate said, "but he's as sick as a dog. All that gallivanting in his weakened state only made mat-ters worse."

"Can I help him now?"

"Go right ahead," Nate said, rising. He stood aside as George rushed to John's aid, then addressed Running An-telope. "I believe you did not harm our friend. But you were all too eager to take his possessions when he was helpless, and this I hold against you. Neither I or my friends have ever sought trouble with your people. We deserve to be treated better than this." He tactfully did not mention the run-in he once had with a war party of five Arapahos who had kidnapped Winona. Fortunately, none of the five made it back to their village to report the clash.

Running Antelope appeared bewildered by the statements. He stared at the minister and the minister's packhorses. "Perhaps we were wrong in thinking this man was our enemy and that we had every right to take his things, but our people have not had many dealings with whites. No one has ever told us the whites are our friends."

"My people have a saying," Nate signed. "Always do to others as you would have them do to you."

"A wise saying," Running Antelope conceded after a bit. "I will be sure to tell everyone I know that your people are not as bad as we think if you allow us to leave in peace."

Nate nodded at their war ponies. "You are free to go now. We have no wish to kill you."

At a gesture from Running Antelope, the Arapahos climbed on their horses and turned their mounts to the south. Running Antelope paused to look at Nate. "You have spared us and we are in your debt. In return, I will warn you that two sleeps ago we came on the sign left by a large war party of Blackfeet. They are roaming in this area."

"I thank you," Nate said, disturbed by the news. If the war party found them, there would be hell to pay. They had to get the reverend back to the Shoshone villages quickly.

Uttering a loud yip, Running Antelope led his fellow warriors southward at a trot. They never looked back, and were soon out of sight.

"Well done, son. You averted bloodshed," Shakespeare stated. "The youngest son of Priam, a true knight, not yet mature, yet matchless, firm of word, speaking in deeds and deedless in his tongue, not soon provoked nor being provoked soon calmed; his heart and hand both open and both free.''

Allen cast an incredulous glance at the mountain man. ''What did you just say?''

''Pay him no mind,'' Nate threw in. ''His brain stopped working a decade ago.''

''You pierce me to the quick, young sire,'' Shakespeare said.

George Burke, who had been carefully examining his brother, turned on them. ''I'm glad you can find the time to joke around while poor John lies at death's door. He's ill, terribly ill, and I don't know what to do.''

Shakespeare slid off his mare. ''Allow me. I've picked up a little medical know-how from the Indians over the years and I might be able to do some good.'' He knelt next to the minister.

''Those Arapahos told us there's a band of Blackfeet in this area,'' Nate informed George. ''No matter how bad off your brother is, we have to head back within the hour. If they caught us here we wouldn't stand a chance.''

''John is in no shape to ride,'' George said.

''Then we'll rig a travois and haul him behind his pack animals,'' Nate proposed.

''Do you really think that will work?'' Allen asked. ''Those horses aren't accustomed to pulling a travois. They might buck or kick or drag Reverend Burke off into the brush before we could stop them.''

''I know,'' Nate said. ''We'll just have to keep them under control until we're satisfied they won't give us any trouble.''

''It sounds too risky to me,'' George said. ''What if I refuse to allow it?''

''Would you rather wind up in the hands of the Blackfeet?'' Nate said, and glanced at the fire. That column of smoke was a certain giveaway of their location, and it would draw a hostile war party like a flame drew moths.

He saw a tin pan the minister had unpacked, apparently in preparation for making a meal, and quickly picked it up and went to the creek. Three trips were needed before he completely doused the flames. He stood back as the last tendrils of smoke climbed upward, then stamped on a few lingering embers.

"We have a problem," Shakespeare announced, standing, his features set in grave lines.

"What is it?" Nate asked, although deep down he had a feeling he already knew.

"Reverend Burke is in bad shape, so bad he won't survive a journey to the Shoshone village even on a travois. I don't know whether the hardships he went through on the plains finally caught up with him or whether he's come down with a sickness. But his fever is burning him up and he's as weak as a newborn kitten." Shakespeare gazed down at the minister and shook his head. "In his weakened state he should never have taken off from the village. He needed another week, at least, to recuperate."

"What do you think we should do then?" Nate inquired.

"Stay here overnight. Give him a chance to get some of his strength back. If we keep him warm and get a lot of liquids into him, he might come around enough to be able to make the trip on a travois."

George squatted and rested a hand on his brother's chest. "I don't care what the rest of you decide, but I'm doing as Mr. McNair says. You can all go back if you want. I'll take care of John."

"We're not about to abandon the two of you," Nate declared. "We'll stay here until morning and see how John is faring."

Allen rested his rifle across his saddle. "The closest hill is west of here," he mentioned, and jabbed a finger at the tree-covered crown visible over the tops of the trees on the other side of the creek. "How about if I ride up there and take a gander at the countryside. If those Blackfeet are skulking about, I might spot them."

"Good idea," Nate said, "Have at it." He watched the trapper ford the creek, then devoted himself to watering and tying their horses while Shakespeare and George did their utmost to make John as comfortable as they could, wrapping the minister in blankets and placing a wet cloth on his brow to cool his perspiring forehead.

George looked around as Nate joined them. "I appreciate you staying," he said, his eyes going past Nate to their mounts. "Say, you didn't unsaddle our horses. Why not?"

"If we have to leave in a hurry there won't be time to spare to saddle up."

"Oh. I hope it doesn't come to that."

"So do I."

Shakespeare was poking a stick among the wet remains of the minister's fire. "I hate to say it, but we'll need a new fire if we're to boil some broth. I'll chop up some jerky and see what else I can find to throw in." He headed into the trees.

"Leave the fire to me," Nate said. "I was the one who put it out in the first place." He walked into the trees and gathered broken limbs he could break down to suitable lengths. The older the limb, the better. As he came into the clearing he saw George holding John's hand and fighting back tears. The two of them must have been very close before the loss of John's wife and son changed John's outlook on life and caused the rift between them.

"Do you have a family in the States?" George asked as Nate walked up.

"Yes."

"Ever miss them?"

"Of course," Nate said, controlling his annoyance at being reminded of them.

"I don't see how you do it," George said earnestly. "I could never sever all my ties with my relatives just to head off for somewhere unknown.'' He stared at the gurgling creek. ''I could never live in these mountains, no matter how splendid they are, knowing I might never see my parents again.''

"Seldom does a day go by that I don't think of my folks and the rest of my kin," Nate said, bending over to deposit the branches on the grass. "We were a close-knit family, and naturally it pained me to leave them." He straightened. "At the time I figured on going back, but things never worked out that way. Now my father and mother are both dead and I'll never be able to look into their faces and tell them how much I truly cared."

George was studying Nate's own face. "I'm sorry. It was thoughtless of me to bring the subject up. I should have realized you'd have regrets."

"Regrets?" Nate said, and sighed. "If you only knew. But there comes a time in a person's life when they have to weigh their personal happiness against the blood ties of their childhood. Sometimes, as in my case, a person finds the mate of their dreams and the land of their heart's desire far from the home they knew and loved, and they have to make the hardest decision of their lives. Do they go off on their own to start anew or return to the old life? Do they stand on their own two feet and do what is best for them or do they do what might be best for their parents?"

"You sound as if—" George began, and stopped abruptly when a tremendous crackling and crashing in the undergrowth on the west bank heralded the sudden arrival of Henry Allen, who galloped into the open and reined up sharply.

"Blackfeet!" Allen cried, pointing to the south. "Heading this way!"

Chapter Seventeen

Hawken in hand, Nate sprinted southward along the edge of the creek where there was scant vegetation and he could make better time. "Stay with your brother," he directed George over his left shoulder. Allen, he saw, had reached their side of the creek and was vaulting to the ground.

Where was Shakespeare?

He couldn't see his mentor anywhere, and he fervently hoped McNair wasn't out in the open where the Blackfeet could see him. Ten feet from the end of the stand of trees he slowed and moved into the pines, doubled at the waist as he glided from trunk to trunk until he could view the approach to the south.

Over a quarter of a mile off was a band of five Blackfeet, hiking northward.

Nate's thumb touched the hammer of his rifle. Between the Hawken and his flintlocks he should be able to drop three of them once they were close enough, but he would rather avoid a conflict if he could. The Blackfeet were concentrating on the ground, reading the sign, and the shod hoof tracks would tell them there were white scalps to be had if they could find where the riders had stopped.

Why were there only five? Nate wondered. The Arapahos had claimed there was a large party. Where were the rest? And speaking of the Arapahos—what had happened to them? Had Running Antelope and his fellows blundered into the Blackfoot war party? Had these five backtracked to determine where the Arapahos came from and stumbled on the tracks left by his party? It hardly seemed possible there had been time for the Blackfeet to kill the four Arapahos. But then he realized 15 to 20 minutes had gone by since the Arapahos had departed, which was plenty of time. In the wilderness death often claimed men and animals alike with astonishing swiftness.

He doubted whether he would ever know the truth. The Blackfeet weren't about to tell him. If he showed himself, they would descend on the stand at a run, thirsting for his blood. At that moment, muffled footsteps to his right let him know he was no longer alone.

"I was only partway up the hill when I saw them through my telescope," Allen disclosed as he crouched behind a fir. "So I came back right away."

"Were these the only ones you saw?" Nate asked.

Allen nodded.

"Did you happen to see Shakespeare?"

"No."

Nate focused on the Blackfeet and came to a decision. "If they come this far we should try to kill them quietly so as not to alert the rest of their war party."

"Two against five? I'm a fair hand with a knife but you're asking the impossible. These are Blackfeet, not Diggers."

The reference was appropriate. Digger Indians were a branch of the Snake tribe to which the Shoshones belonged, but they were as different from the Shoshones as night was from day. While the Shoshones lived much like the other tribes on the plains, the Diggers lived in primitive fashion, going about near naked and subsisting on roots, pine nuts, rice grass, and small game. Most plains tribes held the Diggers in contempt; their fighting prowess was laughed at.

"Even so," Nate said, "if we fire our guns the rest of the war party might hear." He leaned forward, trying to see if the five warriors were carrying firearms. They were still too far off to tell.

"King, look!" Allen suddenly declared, his hand extending to the southeast.

Nate swiveled and felt his pulse quicken. Shakespeare had emerged from another group of trees two hundred yards away and was strolling toward them, his rifle in the crook of his left elbow, his back to the oncoming Blackfeet, oblivious to the danger.

"They see him!" Allen said.

Nate saw that for himself. One of the warriors had excitedly jabbed an arm the second Shakespeare appeared, and now all five were bounding like black-tailed bucks toward the unsuspecting mountain man. They were as far from McNair as he was from the stand, and they were bound to catch him before he reached safety even if he started to run. Nate leaped up and dashed into the open, waving his arms as he did. "Shakespeare! Behind you!" he yelled. "Look behind you!"

The grizzled mountaineer turned. Instead of dashing for the stand, he stuffed something he was holding in his right hand into his ammo pouch, then raised his Hawken and took a bead on the charging Blackfeet.

"He can't hit one at that range," Allen said. "He'll waste the lead."

Nate watched with bated breath. McNair seemed to take forever to aim. At last the Hawken cracked and belched smoke. Down the valley the foremost Blackfoot grabbed at his chest, staggered, then toppled. The rest halted. One of them lifted a rifle. Shakespeare was already sprinting toward the stand, running a zigzag pattern to throw off the warrior's aim.

"He should go to ground," Allen said. "That red devil might get lucky."

The same worry afflicted Nate. He heard a pop when the Blackfoot fired and glanced at Shakespeare, afraid his friend would be hit. Evidently the shot had missed because McNair never slowed. "Keep coming!" Nate called, beckoning his mentor onward.

None of the Blackfeet were in pursuit. All four were gathered around their fallen companion and two of them were assisting the man to his feet. Moments later the pair hastened to the south with their burden as rapidly as they could while the remaining two pivoted and made for the stand.

"They'll try to pin us down here until the rest show up," Allen predicted.

"We can't stay no matter how bad off the minister is," Nate said grimly. As much as he wanted to help John Burke, it was pointless to sacrifice all of their lives in the process. "You go back and set to work on making a travois while I stay and cover Shakespeare."

"George won't like it."

"Tell him that unless we head out in the next ten minutes, we risk being overrun by the Blackfeet."

"All right, but it won't make a difference to him," Allen said, and dashed off.

Nate remained where he was. The two warriors, unwilling to suffer the same fate as their comrade, kept up a halfhearted chase until Shakespeare, panting heavily, reached the trees. Then one bore to the right, the other the left, and they vanished in the high grass and weeds. "Enjoy your stroll?" Nate quipped.

"You have too courtly a wit for me," McNair said,

and grew serious. "Thanks for the warning. I was so busy
thinking about how best to help the reverend that I failed
to pay attention to what was going on around me." He
tapped his temple. " 'Tis gone, you see."

"What is?"

"My brain."

"Quit prattling," Nate said, scanning the valley. "The
Blackfeet will be on us soon. Allen is putting together a
travois, Why don't you lend him a hand while I keep
watch?"

"If we leave now, John Burke will die."

"If we don't, *we'll* die."

"Son, I have an herb that will help him," Shakespeare
said, tapping his ammo pouch. "Give me fifteen minutes
to get the medicine ready, then we can go."

"And what if the Blackfeet get here before you're
done?" Nate responded while backing slowly into the firs.
He alertly scoured the grass for sign of the two warriors
who were in hiding. One had been armed with a lance,
the second a bow, and it was the bowman who most concerned him. The Blackfoot might sneak close enough to
put a shaft into him or one of the others.

McNair also backed into the shelter of the pines. "Bear
with me," he said when they were temporarily safe. "I
found some crawley over yonder, and there's nothing better for fighting high fevers. I can't feed it to Burke as it
is because he's too weak to chew. And tea alone won't
do the job because he needs something more substantial
in his belly. So I'll heat some water, chop up some jerky
into tiny pieces for flavoring, add a smidgen of flour, and
throw in bits of the root. Just one dose of my broth should
have him back on his feet within ten to twelve hours."

Nate knew how effective herbal remedies could be. And
Shakespeare knew more about herbs and wild plants in
general than any white man alive. "Do what you have
to," he said. "I'll stay and keep watch for the war party."

"Thanks," Shakespeare said, giving Nate's arm a squeeze. "I'll fetch you when we're ready." He started to leave.

"Frankly, I never thought you cared that much for ministers," Nate commented. "Some of the remarks you've made led me to believe you hold them in low regard."

The mountain man seemed shocked. "I gave you that impression?" He frowned. "Yes, I suppose I do criticize their profession from time to time, but I have my reasons." Turning, he again began to stride off, then paused and glanced back. "My father was a minister."

"Your father?" Nate blurted out, but Shakespeare was gone, trotting toward the camp. It abruptly dawned on Nate that Shakespeare had never talked about his parents in all the years they had been close friends, had never so much as mentioned their names. Nate did recall a few comments that hinted at a hard childhood and a strict upbringing, but he wouldn't have guessed in a million years that Shakespeare's father had been a man of the cloth.

He leaned against a trunk and scoured the valley. There would be ample opportunity later to probe further into his mentor's background. For now there were the Blackfeet to worry about. Would the entire war party approach from the south, or would they split up and come at the stand from different directions? Should he stay in one spot or rove around the edge of the stand to better safeguard against a surprise attack?

Nate decided to compromise. He moved to a position at the southeast corner where he could see both the southern and eastern approaches. Still not completely satisfied, wishing he had thought to ask Allen for the telescope, he selected a pine and climbed ten feet. His elevated perch gave him a better view of the high grass should the Blackfeet attempt to crawl through it.

Almost immediately he spied the warrior armed with

the lance, lying on his stomach 40 yards out. The bowman, though, was too well concealed.

The minutes elapsed at a snail-like, nerve-racking pace. He heard someone chopping wood at the camp, and figured it was Allen acquiring the poles used to form the framework of the travois. Glancing back, he glimpsed the flickering flames of a fire and Shakespeare kneeling beside it.

More time went by. Nate fidgeted and searched the grass once more. The Blackfoot with the lance had not moved. Nor had the bowman given his location away. They were content to lie there and wait. Nate knew why.

When a half-hour passed and nothing happened, Nate eased toward the ground. He would check to see how the others were doing. The travois should have been put together and the minister fed the broth by now. They should be all set to ride out.

Movement at the south end of the valley made him stop and look. He counted six warriors spread out in a line, coming on at a dogtrot. Only six? He had expected more. Gripping a branch below him, he had started to drop to the earth when he saw additional figures to the east, five of them again spaced at regular intervals as they advanced.

The Blackfeet had split up!

Nate let go and landed hard on his heels. Spinning, he dashed through the trees to the north until the north end of the valley unfolded before his probing gaze. To his consternation, six more Blackfeet were moving toward the stand from that direction. And it was a safe bet there were more warriors coming from the west. Their strategy was obvious; they had the stand hemmed in on all sides, blocking any escape, and they could wage the battle on their own terms.

He raced toward the fire. Shakespeare and Allen were near the horses, talking. One of the pack animals had been fitted with a crude travois consisting of two long poles tied crosswise above the animal's neck and a blanket lashed to the poles dragging on the ground behind it. Lying on that blanket was John Burke, unconscious. George was at the creek, drinking.

All three glanced up as Nate appeared. "We're in for it now," he declared. "The Blackfeet have us surrounded."

Henry Allen cursed. "I knew we were taking too long!" He stared at McNair. "Why didn't you hurry like I wanted?"

"When a man has a job to do, he should do it right," Shakespeare said. "If we rushed building the travois it would fall apart before we went a mile."

George rose, water dripping from his chin. "What do we do?" he asked nervously. "You're the experts. I don't know a thing about Indian fighting."

"We can try to break through their lines, but it won't be easy hauling a travois," Nate said. He addressed his mentor, doing his best to keep any hint of reproach out of his voice. "I trust you fed the broth to the reverend?"

McNair nodded and touched the travois. "He'll pull through, given time."

"Provided we get out of this with our lives," Allen amended, holding his Kentucky in both hands as he peered through the trees. "How many Blackfeet are there anyhow?"

Nate performed a few mental calculations, "Seventeen that I saw, but there are probably more to the west."

"Sweet Jesus!" George Burke exclaimed.

"When this ole boy offered to help you, he didn't count on being killed by a pack of mangy Blackfeet," Allen said.

"We have to stay calm," Shakespeare said. "If we keep our wits about us, we can save our hides." He motioned at the pines on the west side of the creek. "This stand is too big for us to be able to defend the whole thing, so we'll have to pull back into these trees on the east side and hunker down for a battle.''

"How soon before they attack?'' George asked.

"There's no way of telling,'' Nate replied. "But you'll know it when they do.''

"How?''

As if in response, from all points of the compass erupted a savage chorus of bloodcurdling cries.

Chapter Eighteen

"Here they come!" Allen cried.

"You cover George while he takes the horses into the trees!" Shakespeare directed the trapper. "Nate, you head north and I'll go south. Keep moving and make every shot count." With that, he whirled and ran southward.

Nate streaked toward the northeast corner as fast as his legs would carry him. He saw the rows of onrushing Blackfeet before he stopped behind a tree and whipped the Hawken to his shoulder. A strapping warrior waving a huge war club proved a tempting target, and he sent a ball into the man's chest. In a smooth motion he drew his right flintlock, extended it, and fired at a young Blackfoot to the east. The warrior fell, venting a gurgling shriek.

The rest instantly sought cover, diving into the grass.

Crouching, Nate swiftly reloaded, his eyes constantly darting to the north and east. To the south Shakespeare's Hawken boomed, and seconds later Allen's Kentucky thundered close by the creek. Despite the overwhelming odds, they stood a slim chance if they could keep the Blackfeet at bay. Once the warriors got into the pines, the contest would soon be over.

Another factor worked in their favor. Successful war parties were judged not only by how much booty the participating warriors brought back to their village, but by how few men were lost along the way. If a band stole a hundred horses from another tribe, but lost one man in the bargain, that raid was rated a failure and the warrior responsible for leading it was judged to have bad medicine. But if a band stole only ten horses yet didn't lose a single life, that raid was considered a great triumph.

Nate had downed two of the Blackfeet, and they would be averse to losing more. They would try every trick they knew, but they wouldn't recklessly expose themselves again unless certain of slaying him when they did.

Silence prevailed on all sides. He wondered how Shakespeare and Allen had fared. Twisting to scan the stand, he heard a buzzing noise, and threw himself to the right as an arrow streaked past his head and thudded into a fir. He lay on his stomach, his heart drumming, and tried to spot the archer. The high grass taunted him with its seeming emptiness.

Nate crawled backwards until he was next to the wide bole of a tall pine, then rose to his knees. A rifle blasted to the east and a ball smacked into the tree within inches of his face, showering wood slivers on his cheeks and forehead. Dropping flat, he shifted in the hope of spying the warrior, but all he saw was grass.

So that was their game! The Blackfeet were going to lie out there and pick him and his companions off at their convenience. Or worse yet, the Blackfeet would pour arrows and lead into the stand in order to slay the horses, sealing the trap.

A bunch of weeds 20 yards to the north fluttered and a painted face poked out. Nate quickly pointed the Hawken, cocked the hammer, and squeezed the trigger. The Black-foot's head jerked as if kicked by an invisible foot; then the man slumped from sight.

In retaliation three arrows penetrated the stand, all missing by a wide margin.

Nate snaked to the left, convinced only a few of them knew his approximate position. The rest were shooting at random. He sat up behind a fir and hastily reloaded the rifle. As he was sliding the ramrod home, the brush to his rear rustled and George Burke, armed with a flintlock and a knife, stepped from cover. "Get down!" Nate hissed.

George halted, then obeyed, and as he did an arrow flashed through the very space his chest had occupied a second before.

"Stay low!" Nate instructed him.

Nodding, George crawled to the tree. "Shakespeare sent me," he whispered. "He wants to see you. I'll keep watch here."

"Has anyone been hit?"

"Not yet. An Indian almost got me but Allen shot him dead," George said, and smiled. "The really good news is that my brother has revived."

"So soon?"

"The travois bumped into a tree or two when I was getting the horses under cover and all the bouncing around woke him up."

"I'll go see what Shakespeare wants," Nate said. He hesitated, then held out the Hawken. "Take this until I get back. But don't shoot unless you're sure you can score."

"Thanks. I left mine back at the village."

Greenhorns! Nate reflected sourly as he angled through the trees until he came on a small clear space where the horses had been bunched. Shakespeare stood near the travois. "Where's Allen?" Nate inquired.

"On the south side," the mountain man said.

Reverend Burke's eyes were open but they were dull and his eyelids drooped. "Brother King," he said weakly, the words slurred. "How bad off are we? McNair won't tell me."

"Bad enough," Nate said.

"It's all my fault. If I hadn't been so pigheaded—"

"You should rest, Reverend," Nate told him. "You'll need all your strength when we make our escape."

Shakespeare squinted up at the sun. "I reckon we have six hours of daylight left, maybe a little more. Since Blackfeet don't like to fight at night, they'll spend all afternoon trying to kill us one by one, then rush those of us who are left right before dark."

"We'll mount up and be ready to ride when the sun touches the mountains," Nate proposed. "One of us can create a diversion while the rest try to bust through the Blackfoot ring."

"I'll do it."

"No, I will."

"Why you?"

"I have the best horse. Pegasus can move like lightning. They'll never lay a hand on me."

Reverend Burke coughed. "How exactly will you go about diverting their attention?" he asked.

"I don't rightly know yet, but I'll think of something," Nate said, wishing he felt as confident as he sounded. Short of charging the Blackfeet, nothing he could do would occupy their attention long enough for Shakespeare and the rest to flee.

"I wouldn't want your death on my conscience," the minister said. "You're in this fix because of me and it's my responsibility to see to it that all of you get out safely."

"You just lie there and rest," Nate reiterated, puzzled by the reverend's newfound interest in their welfare. It was a trifle late, in his opinion, for Burke to be thinking of them.

From the north came the retort of a rifle.

"George!" Nate declared. "I'll go see why he fired." He was off in a flash, weaving among the trunks, drawing both flintlocks on the run so he would be ready in case the unpredictable Blackfeet had launched a full-scale assault. He saw a commotion under the tree where he had left George, and rounding a thicket discovered the younger Burke in brutal combat with a sturdy Blackfoot. Each had his hands clamped on the other's throat. Nearby lay the Hawken and a lance.

Nate was almost on them before the Blackfoot reacted to his arrival and looked up. The warrior, snarling like an enraged panther, pushed George away and clawed at a big knife in a beaded sheath on his right hip. All Nate had to do was extend his left pistol and fire.

Struck between the eyes, the Blackfoot stiffened, twirled, and pitched forward, striking the tree with a dull thump as he fell.

George put his hands on the ground and started to rise.

"No!" Nate said, crouching and surveying the trees and the valley beyond. "Keep low unless you want an arrow in the back."

"This one nearly had me," George said breathlessly, his face red from his exertions. "I was watching the grass when I heard a faint sound behind me, and there he was."

Nate glanced at the dead warrior. "He was eager to count coup, I reckon."

"Odd thing, though," George whispered. "He didn't try to kill me when he had the chance. My back was to him and he could easily have run me through with his lance, but instead he jumped me and tried to pin me down. Why would he do that?"

"Perhaps he wanted to take you alive. The Blackfeet take particular delight in torturing whites."

George swallowed hard. "I see." He moved to the Hawken and picked it up. "I had the gun cocked when he leaped on me and I'm afraid I accidentally squeezed the trigger.''

"No harm done. I have plenty of black powder and balls," Nate said. Satisfied there were no more Blackfeet lurking close by, he reloaded both the rifle and the pistol. George watched him attentively.

"How can you do that so fast? It would take me two minutes just to measure out the right amount of powder.''

"When you load a gun often enough, you learn shortcuts. You learn how to judge the right amount of powder by sight alone. You always stick the patch between your front teeth until you're done pouring the powder so you can wrap it around the ball that much quicker. And you always start the patch and ball down the barrel with your thumb, then use the ramrod. Shaving a few seconds here and there comes in handy when hostiles are out for your hair.''

George rested a hand on the flintlock tucked under his belt. "I never have been much good with these. Our mother wouldn't allow guns in the house, so I never learned how to properly use them. A friend took me hunting a few times, but I never bagged a deer.''

"If we get out of this, I'll teach you all you need to know," Nate said with a smile. "You'll go back to Rhode Island and bag the biggest buck in the state.''

"That would be something," George said. He glanced toward the clearing where his brother rested on the travois. "Do you need me further? I'd like to check on John.''

"Go right ahead," Nate said, and waited until the younger Burke was gone before he dashed to another tree ten feet away and knelt behind it. To prevent the Blackfeet from pinpointing his position, he could not stay in any one spot too long.

A profoundly disturbing silence enveloped the stand.

Nate listened, but didn't hear so much as a bird. The wildlife had all sought shelter or fled the vicinity. And the breeze had died down so even the high grass was still. He scoured the open tracts and saw nothing. But the Blackfeet were out there, waiting their chance. One mistake and he would pay for it with his life.

Easing onto his stomach, Nate crawled to the west until he could see the creek. The gently flowing, softly bubbling water lent a deceptively tranquil atmosphere to the setting. Sooner or later the Blackfeet would get around to sneaking up on them through the firs on the west side. There were undoubtedly a few concealed in the undergrowth already. If only he could spot one!

Glancing to his left, he spied Henry Allen coming toward him. The trapper moved with fluid grace, like a panther on the prowl, adept at woodland travel, using all available cover.

"I ran into George and he told me you got one of the bastards," Allen whispered as he went prone in the shadow of a thicket.

"Four so far," Nate said.

"Shakespeare has dropped two and I winged one. No wonder they're in no rush to slaughter us." Allen craned his neck upward. "That will change, though, once the sun starts to set."

"We're riding out before they can overwhelm us."

"I know. McNair told me your plan," Allen said, and looked at him. "Listen, friend. I would be grateful if you'll take word to my wife should something happen to me. You can find the Crow village easy enough. Ride for four days due northwest and keep a lookout for a mountain with twin peaks, both covered with snow. There will be a river to the south of that mountain. The Crows are camped beside it."

"Let's pray I won't have to," Nate said.

Branches in the upper half of a pine across the creek suddenly swayed and a bronzed arm appeared, looped over a limb.

"Do you see what I see?" Allen asked, and snickered. "I do."

"Allow me the honor," Allen said, pressing the Kentucky to his shoulder. He grinned as he cocked the hammer.

Nate saw the arm but no other part of the warrior. From the angle the arm was being held, he figured the Blackfoot was lying on the limb. Allen apparently figured the same way, because the next moment the Kentucky boomed and a warrior abruptly sat upright, a hand clutching his side. Grimacing in pain, the Blackfoot doubled over, lost his hold on the limb, and leaned precariously outward.

"Put a ball into him," Allen urged. "Finish him off."

Before Nate could do so, the warrior made a frantic grab at the limb, lost his perch, and plummeted. A high-pitched shriek ended when the Blackfoot slammed into the earth with a sickening crunch.

"That will teach the varmints!" Allen gloated.

As if to prove him wrong, a rifle cracked and a flight of arrows streaked above the creek and into the trees around them, smacking into trunks and limbs. One shaft thumped into the soil within inches of Nate's foot.

Allen laughed. "We've got them riled now!"

The humor was lost on Nate. A second flight of arrows buzzed through the air like angry hornets, and he scooted next to a tree for protection. A shaft hit the front of the trunk, shattering instead of imbedding itself.

"Show yourselves, you yellow-bellies," Allen growled as he fed black powder into his rifle. "I want another shot. Just one is all I ask."

Nate saw a third swarm of arrows speed toward them. He had turned to say that the thicket was a poor shield, and to advise the trapper to find better shelter, when suddenly a shaft sped true.

Henry Allen was hit.

Chapter Nineteen

The arrow caught the trapper on the right side above the thigh, piercing him from front to back, the impact twisting him around. Allen grunted, grabbed the shaft, and sprawled onto his side, his features contorted in agony.

"Hang on!" Nate said, reaching Allen in two bounds and stepping over the lanky frontiersman to grasp him under the arms. Digging in his heels, he heaved, and dragged Allen away from the thicket as more shafts sought them. Several tightly spaced pines afforded sanctuary.

"It hurts like the dickens," Allen rasped after Nate lowered him to the ground. Although in torment, he had held onto the Kentucky, which he now put beside him. "Damn them all to hell."

Nate sank on one knee. Thankfully, the arrow had penetrated skin and flesh but missed the lower ribs. The barbed arrowhead jutted six inches from the exit wound, which in itself was a stroke of luck. Indians sometimes applied snake venom or other poisons to the tips of their shafts, and an arrowhead left in the body for any length of time could result in death even though it missed vital organs. Another reason trappers had to dig out arrowheads quickly was that the glue holding the arrowheads on the shafts often dissolved after 20 or 30 minutes. If a man didn't get the head out before it came off, he would be forced to dig around inside with a knife or a special pair of thin pliers many trappers carried for just such an emergency.

"You know what to do," Allen said, and bit his lower lip.

"First things first," Nate said, and peered past the pines. The Blackfeet had vented their anger and were holding their fire. None were visible. Shifting, he searched around until he located a piece of broken branch as long as his middle finger and as thick as his thumb. This he gave to Allen.

"If I pass out I'll never stand the shame," the trapper said. He stuck the piece in his mouth and clamped down.

"Here we go," Nate said, gripping the shaft below the arrowhead and bracing his other hand against Allen's back over the exit wound, his finger curled over the arrow. Allen nodded once. Nate bunched his shoulder muscles, then wrenched with all his might.

The arrow broke with a loud snap.

Nate tossed the barbed tip aside and moved in front of the trapper. Allen's brow was beaded with perspiration and saliva flecked his lips. "Can you take it?" Nate asked.

Brief anger animated Allen's eyes. Free trappers prided themselves on their fortitude and their ability to endure pain without complaint. There were cases where men had been terribly mauled by grizzlies or been severely hurt battling hostiles, yet they'd never voiced a single complaint. Some, who hadn't been able to extract a deeply imbedded arrowhead, carried the grisly memento inside of them for years before they came on someone with enough surgical skill to remove it. Allen impatiently motioned for Nate to proceed.

"Hold on," Nate said, and again checked the trees across the creek for signs of the Blackfeet. He also scanned the north and east perimeter. The war party was still biding its time. Kneeling, he grasped the shaft next to Allen's buckskin shirt, then pulled. While arrows frequently came out easily, on other occasions they were as hard to remove as a contrary wisdom tooth. This shaft was difficult to budge. He had to twist it slightly to work it loose, and keep twisting to get it to continue sliding out inch by slow inch.

Allen's body shook, his teeth digging into the branch, his fists clenched on his lap.

"It's coming," Nate said, trying not to think of the fact his back was to the edge of the trees, and trying not to imagine what would happen should a Blackfoot spot him. He would be a sitting duck. The hair at the nape of his neck tingled the whole time he tugged on the arrow. When, at long last, the shaft popped free, blood dripping from the broken end, he promptly turned to look for hostiles. He saw only firs and brush.

Henry Allen spat out the branch, which had nearly been bitten in two, and gingerly touched his right side. "Thanks," he said. He inhaled deeply and mopped his forehead.

"We should get you to the clearing," Nate proposed, retrieving his Hawken.

"I can manage by my lonesome. You stay here in case those varmints try something."

"Are you sure?"

"Quit babying me, King. I'm a growed man, not a kid," Allen said, rising until he was stooped over, the Kentucky in his right hand. "Damned if you don't act like a mother hen sometimes." Chuckling, he made his way to the south.

Nate found himself liking the trapper a lot. Once they escaped—if they did—he intended to invite Allen and Allen's wife to the Shoshone village. The Crows and the Shoshones got along tolerably well so there shouldn't be a problem in that regard.

He crept to within eight feet of the tree line. Propped on his elbows, he surveyed the valley. What if the Blackfeet didn't wait until sunset? What if they sprang their trap sooner? Getting the reverend to safety would be a hopeless task; simply staying alive would be a chore. But if he was to mount Pegasus right then and there and cut out at a full gallop, he'd more than likely make it through the Blackfeet. There was only one problem. He would have to leave the others behind, and he would never, ever desert friends in a time of dire need.

For the next two hours Nate patrolled the north end of the stand, going from east to west and back again, stealthily slipping from tree to tree, always alert, always ready to fire should a Blackfoot appear. He felt disappointed when none did.

The sun arced on its downward course through the blue vault of the sky.

Nate was trying to determine if a dark patch off in the grass was a weed or a warrior when someone came through the brush to his rear and whispered urgently.

"King! Shakespeare wants all of us at the clearing."

Glancing over a shoulder, Nate saw the younger Burke. George was a bundle of nervous energy, and kept transferring his weight from one foot to the other while wagging the flintlock he held as if swatting at flies. "Why? What's wrong?" Nate asked.

"We're pulling out now instead of waiting for sunset."

Surprised, Nate cautiously retreated until he stood by Burke's side. "Why the change in plans?"

"Talk to Shakespeare. He told me the Blackfeet are up to something but he didn't say what."

Alarmed, Nate hastened to the clearing. All the horses were facing due south and Henry Allen was astride the roan, holding the leads to the pack animals. McNair was adjusting the bridle on his white mare. Reverend Burke, amazingly, was sitting up, a bible in his left hand. "How are you faring?" Nate inquired.

"As well as can be expected. Don't fret over me, brother. The Lord will preserve me."

Nate stepped to the mare. "Why the rush to get out of here? I thought we were waiting until near dark."

"I took Henry's telescope and climbed a tree," Shakespeare answered. "Spotted six warriors sneaking to the west to reinforce those already there. The way I see it, they're getting set to mount an attack. If they come at us through the trees on the other side of the creek, they'll force us out into the grass where the rest can kill us or take us prisoner."

"Damn," Nate muttered, although he admired the wily strategy. When would he learn to never underestimate the Blackfeet? When would he learn to always expect them to do the unexpected? How often must he remind himself they were the scourge of the northern plains and Rockies with good reason?

"If most of the warriors are west of us, their lines in the grass will be thin," Shakespeare was saying. "We should be able to fight our way out." He finished with the bridle. "We need to leave now, before they can spring their surprise. I'll go first to draw their fire. Allen will handle the pack animals. George will stick close to the travois so he can keep an eye on his brother. You bring up the rear."

"I should be the one who draws their fire," Nate objected. "I can—" He stopped speaking as a series of savage whoops arose west of the creek.

"They're attacking!" Allen cried. "And they'll be on us before we can get out of the stand!"

"I'll hold them off!" Nate said, whirling. He ran toward the creek, cocking the Hawken as he did, and probed the trees for movement. If he could delay the Blackfeet, if he could halt the charge for even a few minutes, it would give the others the time they needed to escape. The ribbon of water came into view, and so did a dozen or more Blackfeet who had already crossed it and were entering the pines on the east side. Stopping, he jammed the stock to his shoulder, sighted, and stroked the trigger.

The Hawken spat lead and smoke. A tall Blackfoot who seemed to be leading the attack crumpled. Immediately, the rest sought cover, some diving to the ground, others dashing behind trees. But a few never made it.

To the left of Nate guns cracked, three in swift succession, and he turned to see Shakespeare, Allen, and George, smoke curling from the barrels of their weapons. "What the—!" he blurted out, and saw a warrior coming straight at him bearing an upraised war club. In the blink of an eye the right flintlock was in his hand, and he fired when the onrushing Blackfoot was no more than seven feet away. The ball took the warrior in the throat, stopping him in his tracks as if he had slammed into a stone wall. Then the Blackfoot staggered and fell to his knees, his hands clamped to the wound in a futile attempt to staunch the crimson geyser spraying forth.

Nate would have liked to finish the warrior off, but if he used the second flintlock he would have to rely on his knife or tomahawk should another Blackfoot try to slay him. So he backed up, sticking the expended pistol under his belt and drawing the loaded one.

To the left more guns boomed. Shakespeare and Allen fired pistols simultaneously while retreating into the brush.

Suddenly someone screamed.

Pivoting, Nate beheld George Burke on his side on the ground, an arrow through his chest. Nate took a step, intending to drag Burke to safety, when two more shafts sped out of the greenery and sliced into Burke's chest within a hand's width of the first.

George swiveled his head and spied Nate. His eyes were wide in shock and disbelief. Then, blubbering red spittle, he collapsed and expired with a sigh.

Pausing behind a fir, Nate scanned the stand. The Blackfeet were all in hiding. Temporarily, at least, the charge had been broken. Both Shakespeare and Allen were behind trunks, reloading. Crouching low, he burst from concealment, racing toward McNair. A rifle thundered and something tugged at his beaver hat. An arrow missed his head by a hair. And then he was there, the trunk sheltering him.

"Trying to get yourself killed, Horatio?" Shakespeare whispered while wedging a ball and patch into his rifle.

"What the hell are you doing? You were supposed to cut out with the others."

"Does your wife know you use such foul language?"

"Damn it, this is no time to be making jokes."

"Why, how now, Adam! no greater heart in thee? Live a little; comfort a little; cheer thyself a little."

"Shakespeare!"

The mountain man grinned and peeked around the pine. "All right. All right. Don't throw a fit." He glanced at Nate. "Did you really and truly think I would run off and leave you to be butchered? I knew what you were trying to do, but one man couldn't stem their charge. So we joined in. Now, if they don't press us, we can sneak back to the horses and light out." He gazed into the trees. "Where's George?"

"He's dead."

"Drat. I liked the lad." Shakespeare leaned the rifle against the trunk and began reloading his pistol. "You'd better reload your pieces, Horatio, unless you're fixing on fighting the Blackfeet tooth and claw."

Exasperated, Nate opened his powder horn. "I don't need you to remind me what to do. And I'll thank you to stop calling me Horatio. It's not my name.''

"What's in a name? That which we call a rose by any other name would smell as sweet.''

"Sometimes I think you're a lunatic,'' Nate muttered. He repeatedly glanced at the surrounding pines, anticipating a second assault.

"We'll let them try again,'' Shakespeare whispered loud enough for Allen to hear. "When they hunt their holes, we get back to the horses and show these Blackfeet how fast white men can ride when they have to.''

"We can't go fast hauling that travois,'' Nate reminded him. "The Blackfeet will be on us like wolves on snowbound deer.''

"We are not the first who with best meaning have incurred the worst.''

"Here they come!'' Allen warned.

Flitting like painted specters from spot to spot, yipping and yelling like demented furies, the warriors were closing in, some sweeping to the right, some to the left, executing a pincer movement to outflank their foes.

"Fire, men, fire!'' Shakespeare bellowed, doing just that. About 30 feet out a Blackfoot toppled, a hole where his nose had been.

Nate heard Allen join the fray as he picked up the loaded flintlock, trained it at an onrushing figure, and shot. A feather in the warrior's hair leaped from the man's head, but the Blackfoot himself, untouched, dove for safety.

"Now!'' Shakespeare shouted, backing into the undergrowth.

All of Nate's guns were empty and taking the precious time necessary to reload them would be certain suicide; the Blackfeet would be on him before he could do it, So he sprinted for the clearing, dodging and weaving like a man possessed, deadly shafts tipped with their terrible barbed points raining down on all sides. Shakespeare was ahead of him. Allen, because of his wound, was in the rear but moving as if his heels were on fire.

Nate saw Shakespeare break from the vegetation into the clearing, and a second later did likewise, only to halt in astonishment and gap in stupefied shock at finding their horses gone. Every last animal. Even the packhorses and the travois. ''How?'' he blurted.

''There!'' McNair declared, pointing to the south.

Nate, bewildered, sprang forward. Outlined against the firs, standing at the boundary of the stand and the tall grass, were all the animals including Pegasus. How had they gotten there? Was the reverend responsible? To the west the Blackfeet whooped in murderous rage as they closed in.

The travois was empty.

In startled bewilderment Nate noticed the vacant blanket and feared the Blackfeet had seized the minister, until his gaze lifted and he spied Reverend John Burke walking into the grass. ''Reverend!'' he yelled, but Burke paid no heed. The minister, walked with firm tread, his shoulders squared, his bible held aloft in his right hand.

Nate stopped beside Pegasus and surveyed the valley. The Blackfeet in the grass had yet to show themselves. Their attention was undoubtedly on the reverend, who suddenly started quoting Scripture at the top of his lungs.

''The Lord is my shepherd, I shall not want. He maketh me to lie down in green pastures, he leadeth me beside the still waters.''

''Come back!'' Nate cried. He took a step to go after Burke, but a firm restraining hand on his arm checked his advance.

''No!'' Shakespeare said. ''Mount and ride. We'll get him on the fly.''

Nate spun and vaulted onto his stallion. Out in the open the minister boldly walked deeper into the grass, reciting all the while.

''He restoreth my soul. He leadeth me in the paths of

righteousness for his name's sake. Yea, though I walk through the valley of the shadow of death, I will fear no evil for thou art with me. Thy rod and thy staff they comfort me.''

Jabbing his heels into Pegasus, Nate galloped toward John Burke. A Blackfoot popped up off to the right, an arrow nocked to a taut bowstring, and aimed at the too tempting target. ''Try me!'' Nate shouted, but the warrior loosed the shaft a heartbeat later, and in helpless horror Nate witnessed the flight of the glittering arrow as it flew true, striking the reverend high on the chest.

John Burke staggered and almost fell. Miraculously, he regained his balance, held the bible higher, and walked onward. ''Thou preparest a table before me in the presence of mine enemies,'' he thundered as if from a pulpit. ''Thou anointest my head with oil; my cup runneth over.''

Nate was halfway to the minister. He saw the Blackfoot nock another shaft, and nearly laughed with glee when Henry Allen's Kentucky cracked and the warrior dropped like a stone. His elation was short-lived, however.

Another Blackfoot rose, his right arm sweeping back to throw a lance.

This time it was Shakespeare who fired. The warrior was lifted from his feet and crashed from sight in the grass.

''Reverend Burke!'' Nate called, hunching over, bracing to grab the minister under an arm and heave him over the saddle. Vaguely he was aware of Blackfeet in the trees behind them and a few Blackfeet on both sides.

''Surely goodness and mercy shall follow me all the days of my life,'' the minister roared, ''and I will dwell in the house of the Lord forever!'' Stopping, he turned, his eyes alighting on Nate, each twinkling with a gleaming spark of inner victory. He beamed proudly. ''Did you see, brother?'' he yelled. ''Did you see?''

See what? Nate wondered, reaching out with his left hand. He was nearly there—ten feet or less to go and he could grasp the reverend's arm—when another arrow transfixed John Burke from back to front, the tip exploding out Burke's chest. The reverend took a halting step, gawked at the barbed point coated red with his blood, and then collapsed, falling straight down in a disjointed heap.

"No!" Nate bellowed, slowing, thinking there still might be hope, that John Burke might still be alive, until a glimpse of the minister's blank eyes and parted lips convinced him otherwise. Glancing up, he spotted the warrior responsible whipping another arrow from a quiver. Rage seized him, and without realizing what he was doing he goaded Pegasus into a full gallop and angled toward the bowman.

The Blackfoot nocked the arrow and elevated the bow, his actions precise and rapid, a seasoned warrior who knew enough not to waste motion when in combat. He made no effort to move out of the way until the absolute last moment.

Nate's gaze was locked on his adversary. When the arrow leaped toward him he was rigid in the saddle, aflame with a burning desire to revenge John Burke. He scarcely felt the shaft as it shot under his left arm, clipping fringe as it passed. But he did feel the impact when Pegasus plowed into the Blackfoot like a living battering ram and sent the warrior flying. The bow sailed into the grass. Nate wheeled his stallion, holding the Hawken and the reins in one hand, and drew his tomahawk. Somewhere, someone was shouting. He didn't care who or why. All he cared about was satisfying his craving for vengeance.

The stallion pounded toward the warrior once more. Dazed but game, the Blackfoot was standing, pulling a sheath knife as he straightened. He never had the opportunity to use it.

Nate swooped down on the warrior, his tomahawk shining in the sunlight as he swung it on high, then buried the edge in the top of the Blackfoot's skull. He let go of the handle and swept on past, making for the south end of the valley, hearing rifles blast and the frenzied cries of the war party.

Somehow, Shakespeare and Allen had gotten ahead of him and were beckoning him on.

He raced after them, listening to the buzz of arrows and balls, hoping Pegasus would be spared. A glance showed him ten or so Blackfeet pouring from the pines. He wasn't worried. Not even the fleetest of men could hope to overtake a robust stallion in the prime of its life.

Shortly the arrows and balls ceased cleaving the air and Nate slowed Pegasus to a trot. A hundred yards distant awaited his friends. Twisting, he saw a crowing Blackfoot next to John Burke, waving the minister's scalp in small circles. Had the Hawken been loaded he would have shot the warrior dead. He watched others dance in glee around the body and strike it with their clubs and tomahawks. Still others had hold of the packhorses and the animals belonging to the Burke brothers, but they were making no attempt to give chase. Evidently the Blackfeet were satisfied with their spoils, or else they simply didn't care to lose any more men.

"I thought for a bit there you were a goner, King."

Facing front, Nate thoughtfully regarded the trapper and fell in between Allen and McNair as they started homeward. "It would have served me right if I was." He sighed and sadly shook his head. "I came so close. So damn close."

"Don't talk nonsense, Horatio," Shakespeare said. "We did all we could for the good reverend, and then some. He made the choice. There was nothing we could do."

"What choice?" Allen asked. "Do you mean he wanted to get himself killed? He deliberately walked on out there knowing what would happen?"

"Stranger things have happened."

Nate breathed the sweet mountain air and watched a butterfly flutter over the grass. "I'll find a way to send word to the Burke family in Rhode Island. It's the least I can do." He looked toward the Blackfeet again, to be certain none were in pursuit. The war party was moving into the stand, taking Burke's body with them.

Henry Allen was also gazing back at the trees. "I still don't understand. Why did Reverend Burke do it?"

"Old William S. had the answer to that one," McNair responded soberly. "All the world's a stage, and all the men and women merely players. They have their exits and their entrances. And one man in his time plays many parts." He gave the mare a pat. "I just pray, when my times comes, I play my part as well as John Burke did."

SPECIAL SNEAK PREVIEW!

NEW SERIES!
CHEYENNE

#1: ARROW KEEPER
by Judd Cole

Set on the Western frontier before the Civil War, *Cheyenne* follows the perilous adventures of young Matthew Hanchon as he fights to make himself a free man. Born Indian, raised white, Matthew has never known anything but fear and distrust among the settlers. But when he tries to find his place among his own people, he discovers that the Cheyenne hate him as much as the whites. He'll need a frontiersman's cunning and grit and a warrior's courage, strength, and skill— or he'll never survive!

COMING IN SEPTEMBER TO BOOKSTORES AND NEWSSTANDS EVERYWHERE!

OUR STORY SO FAR...

Adopted by a childless white couple after his tribe was slaughtered, Matthew Hanchon has never felt truly accepted by many of the pioneers. When his parents' mercantile store is threatened by his enemies, the youth decides to find his place among his own people. But from his first encounter with other Cheyenne, Matthew discovers that he faces a struggle that may end with his own bloody death!

The oldest brave rode close enough to touch the bay's nose. He said something in a strange language that was mere gibberish to the youth.

Unsure what to do, Matthew finally offered his right hand. "How do you do?" he said. "My name is Matthew Hanchon."

The brave stared at the hand, contempt starched into every feature. Behind him, the others broke into gales of hearty laughter.

"How do you do?" one of them said awkwardly, offering his hand to another. Both braves laughed so hard they had to slide down from their horses and roll on the ground.

As his friends laughed, the brave who had ridden forward allowed his face to show his hatred for the Indian who had traded his breechclout and moccasins for trousers and boots. He wheeled his pony around and returned to his companions. After a brief conference, the youngest Cheyenne rode forward.

"I am called Wolf Who Hunts Smiling," he said proudly in slow but good English. "My father was Red Feather of the Panther Clan. I belong to Yellow Bear's band."

"You speak English!" said Matthew, relieved.

"For two winters, I and my father were prisoners of the Long Knives at the soldier's house called Fort Laramie. We escaped, but my father was killed by the big-talking guns."

His words were as flat and hate-filled as his eyes. "Why have you ridden into our country?" he demanded.

Matthew swallowed the hard lump in his throat. For the first time he finally had to admit his purpose. "Because I am a Cheyenne, and I want to be with my own people."

A sneer divided Wolf Who Hunts Smiling's face. He called something back over his shoulder to the rest, and they laughed again.

"You, a *Shaiyena!*" said Wolf Who Hunts Smiling. "You who offer us your hand to shake like the Bluecoat liars who shake the red man's hand before they kill him and take his land? I say you are a double-tongued spy sent to listen and learn. Everyone knows that the Bluecoats use Indian spies to discover our camps."

"No! I swear I'm not."

"I have no ears to hear your lies, white man's dog!"

Wolf Who Hunts Smiling abruptly wheeled his pony around and approached his companions again. After a brief exchange with the other braves, he returned, his eyes glinting with triumph.

"I told them you are a spy who pretends not to know our language. The rest agree."

Without another word Wolf Who Hunts Smiling leaned forward, hugging his mustang's neck between his knees. To Matthew's surprise, he slid the new Colt out of the saddle scabbard.

When Matthew instinctively reached out to grab the weapon back, Wolf Who Hunts Smiling brought the buttstock up hard against the side of the youth's head. He saw a quick burst of bright orange then he slid down out of the saddle like a heavy bag of grain.

Matthew never quite lost consciousness, but his limbs felt like stones he could not lift. Helpless, he watched from the ground as the Cheyenne crowded around his horse and divided up everything he owned, the oldest Indian doing the distributing. After a brief speech, the brave handed the Colt to Wolf Who Hunts Smiling.

. . .

Without a word, Wolf Who Hunts Smiling calmly lifted the rifle and shot the bay in the head. The animal just missed crushing Matthew as it crumpled to the ground, blood blossoming out of its skull. When Matthew cried out, Wolf Who Hunts Smiling dismounted and pressed a razor-sharp knife against his neck.

"It has been decided. I may kill the spy to avenge my father!"